Secrets

Way Beyond the Sky, Where Dragons Rule, Volume 4

Jeri Andrew

Published by Jeri Andrew, 2023.

This is a work of fiction. Similarities to real people, places, or events are entirely coincidental.

SECRETS

First edition. November 3, 2023.

Copyright © 2023 Jeri Andrew.

ISBN: 979-8223529583

Written by Jeri Andrew.

Table of Contents

Huge thanks to Drew, who, made this adventure possible.

A special thanks to all of my friends lending their names and likenesses for use with the characters.

Tootsie, Chathey Ann, Merrill, Lee, and so many more! Thank you for being a part of this adventure!

Chapter 1

AlaHanDrea was having her morning swim, thinking about the Mers and how badly she missed them, and everyone else too.

Years were passing... sometimes the loneliness was a bit overwhelming. Oh, she had company enough, just not the company she longed for.

She had no idea who had survived and who had not. She used to get visits from Alexa, but even she had not been around in ages.

Her mind wandered over to the day Alexa had come into her life... evacuating her to that island to save her.... AlaHanDrea couldn't figure out why she had to be evacuated separately from Isabel and the rest of her friends. She couldn't even reach Mr. Jax, Raynar or Healix...

She had been so upset over Leon that she didn't object, she went with Alexa as requested....

It had been so, so long since she had seen anyone from her life before the island. She couldn't even remember how old she was now. Time had little meaning where she was.

Well, at least she had no worries of losing her virginity during her teen years!

She had tried to leave on more than one occasion, but wasn't able to. That electromagnetic disturbance had made leaving impossible.

Least wise, leaving by way of magic...

The thing she missed most was human meals... the people on her island were not for dinner....

AlaHanDrea hoped beyond hope that Alexa was alive and well.

The islands native population was interesting, to say the least. She was living among mimics... strange creatures mimics... they would look at you, then look like you! They would take memories and knowledge as well as looks. There were days she'd see herself all over the island....

It was a hard thing to get used to, for sure. None of them wanted to get too close to her, they were afraid of her.

Surely the pandemic responsible for her being evacuated to the island was getting under control by now... she'd been there for so, so long!

Mimics were very powerful creatures! Almost as powerful as she was! Not quite, but almost....

Judging from the changes in her body, AlaHanDrea was guessing that she was around 18 or maybe even 20!

"GEORGE, HAS THE GUARD found Brad Lee yet?" Isabel asked.

"Yes, they are bringing him in. They said that he is a new father and has been away because he was hatching eggs." George explained.

"Are they bringing his children, too?"

"Well, of course, they couldn't very well leave the children alone. I've already called the boys."

"What about the children's mother?"

"They made no mention of the mother. Just Brad Lee and his kids..."

"Hmmm, this ought to be an interesting meeting..."

Isabel had several she dragons take charge of the children for Brad Lee, while the meeting was taking place.

"Is AlaHanDrea coming? Is Keithen coming? Has anyone seen either of them? George, have you attempted to summon AlaHanDrea?" Isabel asked.

"I have tried, yes. I think I will summon our son, instead..."

"Hello father, you called?" Keithen asked.

"Yes, Keithen, have you seen AlaHanDrea?"

"Not today, I haven't. Back at Braynar's new home, she put some kind of spell on me. That's o.k, because I realized it and got outta there!"

"What the Hell are you talking about, son? She didn't put a spell on you!"

"Yes... she did! Y'all saw her do it! When she kissed me then slapped me!"

"Son, that's called foreplay! The only spell cast is called horny! She turned you on! That's not magic, it's hormones! Keithen, what have you done now?"

"Well, when I left the cave after she slapped me, I went outside and asked her to please come talk to me, asked her to forgive me and told her that I loved her, no matter what she looked like. She showed up, wiping my tears with a soft cloth and I kissed her! Then, I picked her up and flew her to my lair... we didn't go inside, we just laid in the hammock. I had every intention on being good, but dad, she started it!

She was all kissing on my neck, running her hands all over me, then she reached down and began rubbing my... uh, well, she began rubbing me through my pants!

Dad, I'm a healthy young male! I tore her clothes off and spent a few hours , uh... well, then, we fell asleep in each other's arms. When I woke up, I realized the truth and got the hell out of there before she woke up!"

"You've got to be kidding me.... Keithen! What am I going to do with you? I know what I'm going to do with you, you're going back to Pooky's."

"But... dad..."

"Don't you butt dad, me! Keithen, shame on you, son! That poor girl. I'm going looking for her. You stay here with your mother and brother and help figure out this whole Brad Lee thing. I'll be back... my own son!!!"

"AlaHanDrea! Sweetheart, it's George, are you up here still."

George found her laying on the ground, passed out. Her face was swollen from crying. He felt so ashamed of Keithen when he found her like that.

George couldn't believe how beautiful she was! Laying nude in the grass... "my son is an idiot!" He said out loud to himself.

He picked her up off of the ground, holding her in his arms like he would a baby. Her head laid against his chest, she wrapped her arms around his neck. George carried her over to the hammock, then thought better of it and used his magic to make a bed to lay her in. He laid her down, but she didn't want to let go of his neck, so he laid down next to her and held her in his arms. She snuggled right up against him.

It felt so good to be held, she didn't want to let go. No words were spoken. Not by her, anyway.

George began singing to her as he held her, stroking her cheeks with his fingers, brushing the hair away from her face.

She finally opened her eyes and gazed into his eye... the next thing George knew, he was kissing her. He didn't plan it, didn't really mean for it to happen, but laying in a bed next to her all naked like that... he found himself kissing her and really liking it.... She didn't resist at all.... She responded as though it was the natural thing to do.... Being with him like that... she put her hands inside of his shirt so she could feel his bare skin, then helped him to take his shirt off. The feel of their bare skin touching was driving him wild!

Desire filled him like it hadn't done in years, no, decades! All good sense left him... he became driven by desire... he had gone to her to comfort her... he hadn't meant to do it, he just couldn't help himself!

She was right there! And so beautiful and so naked!

No man could have resisted her!

He finally gave up trying to resist... it was pointless...

George couldn't believe himself! It was as if he were a young man dragon again! He hadn't lasted like that since he was very young!

The intensity was incredible! Nothing else mattered but the two of them in those moments...

They finally laid in each other's arms, basking in the after glow... George didn't know what to say... he didn't know what to think, either. The reality of it all was beginning to set in... he was beginning to feel like he had taken advantage of her, knowing full well she was in deep pain...

"Thank you, George. You sweet, precious, man! George, no one needs to know other than you and I. It's no one else's business but our own. I needed you more than words can say. Please, just hold me for a little while longer. I'm not quite ready for this to end..."

Her words were soothing, just what he needed to hear. He had desired her for a very long time, he just never acted on it. She was thanking him! The worry began to fade...

"George, please, kiss me again..." she said, more as a question. He leaned up, looked into her eyes, then kissed her very lovingly. The kiss turned passionate and heat began to build once more! He couldn't help himself! It was as if he hadn't had any in weeks! Before he realized what he was doing, they were once again lost in one another.... The heat rose to unbelievable heights! He had finished two more times before finally stopping. Not since he was a very young dragon, had he gone so many times in a row! Especially twice non stop! Twice non stop after going three times back to back! Yet, strangely enough, he felt energized! Stronger... more powerful... ....

"AlaHanDrea, baby girl, I need you to come back with me. Please.

I know you don't think anyone else needs to know, but, I'm married, sweetie. My wife and I have no secrets. Not anymore, anyway. I mean, my wives and I,

have no secrets and I won't lie to them. I'm not going to walk in broadcasting it, but I'll not lie, either."

"But I don't wish for them to know, George. If you're going to tell them, then I won't go back. I don't want Isabel to know what I've done! And I especially don't want Braynar, Keithen and Danalli to know! Please George, don't tell them! I'm begging you, please!"

"I agree, no one needs to know, no one but Isabel..."

"Why Isabel?"

"Because she's my wife, she has a right to know! If I keep it from her, then I am guilty of betrayal."

"Oh. Then, please bring her here, right now, just her..."

"O.k., I'm good with that. Isabel! Isabel! Come here please, Isabel! Now!"

"Yes, George? Hello, AlaHanDrea, how are you, baby girl?"

"Naked. I'm naked. I seduced George. He came to comfort me because Keithen is a jerk and an ass and I seduced him. I could have used magic to clothe myself, but I chose to remain nude, then removed his shirt while he was trying to comfort me. I took advantage of him and his kind nature. I screwed his brains out..."

"Well, George, did you enjoy it?"

"Ya, I sure did! It was actually an awesome experience."

"Do you both feel better?"

"Ya, I know I do," George replied.

"Ya, me too."

"O.k., then, what's the issue?"

"Isabel... I love you!" AlaHanDrea told her, than gave her a big hug, naked.

Isabel got to experience first hand what it was like to hold AlaHanDrea's bare body and instantly understood ...

"Girl! Wow! You are irresistible! Let's get some clothes on you!"

The clothes AlaHanDrea chose to put on covered very little of her body. The top covered her nipples. The bottom sort of covered her crotch and the center of her ass... her top was nothing more than 2 inch straps making a cross cross over her boobs and around her neck. She put on knee moccasins and was ready to go. Isabel put a flowing sheer white gown on her as a compromise.

"Girly, if we don't cover you just a little, we won't make it out of here!" She said with a chuckle.

"Do y'all know why Keithen hurt me again? Why'd he do it?"

"Because my son is an ass. He got it in his head that you used magic against him."

"Seriously? Well, I didn't! I can! But I didn't! Well, if I'm paying for it, I may as well do it!" She said, with a determination in her voice.

THE THREE OF THEM RETURNED to the meeting. AlaHanDrea was glad to see that Keithen was already there. she had plans for him!

Oh, yes, she sure did! Not really one to resort to spells, she made an exception, casting a love spell on Keithen that made him follow her around, like a little puppy dog, panting after her.

George and Isabel let it slide for a few hours, then broke the spell on their son, blocking her ability to do it again.

She could have broken past their magic, but didn't out of respect for them both. Anyway, she was becoming nervous about her secret being revealed!

She already knew that Braynar suspected something was Amiss.

Chapter 2

"So, boys, what have we determined what happened... ? Isabel asked Braynar.

"Well, Brad Lee swears up and down that he didn't see her after she ran from the dance floor, after seeing Dane and his wife on the big screen... and Keithen and his lady on the dance floor.

But, when I replay videos of the night, you can clearly see him making chase when she runs off..." Danalli told Isabel.

"Who is the mother to the children?"

"He isn't answering us."

"Bring him to me. Now. Right now."

"Yes, mother."

"AlaHanDrea, sweetie, please replay your memories for us. Go ahead, it's o.k.." Isabel instructed.

AlaHanDrea did as she was told, reluctantly... there were obvious glitches in the replay, indicating they'd been messed with!

Raynar entered and took over.

He placed his hand on her head and the memories began to come into true focus... they all watched while BradLee manhandled Baby Girl... they watched as he drugged her and held her prisoner, then saw him take the eggs from her... they watched every detail, down to him leaving her laying in the dirt, robbed of her eggs and her memories... unconscious and vulnerable....

Isabel ordered the children be brought in. Raynar took a close look at the babies and took Isabel off to the other room...

"Isabel, that's not AlaHanDrea! That's not Baby Girl! "

"What? What you saying? What do you mean?"

"I mean, it's an imposter! It's a mimic!"

"Oh no, you're kidding, right?

"I wish that I were!"

"Well, where is AlaHanDrea?"

"If I had to guess, I'd say she's being help prisoner on Mimic Island in the south seas, or there about. I doubt they killed her. Mimics love to experience others lives... They are powerful, strange creatures..."

"I wonder how long this mimic has been pretending to be AlaHanDrea?"

"Well, when did she stop flying off into battle as if she could fight the war all by herself?"

"OMG! That long? Raynar, what do we do? "

"Well, we can't let on that we know. We have to go along with the charade for now. Keep this to yourself... For as long as you can... I may try to force her hand... Let me to talk to Jax and Healix. "

"Well, sure, o.k. that's fine. So, what do you think is the goal of this mimic creature?"

"You might say the mimic is her biggest fan! It wants to be her!"

"Oh."

"Isabel, make it to where her and I are alone together... "

"O.k."

"AlaHanDrea, this dragon, Brad Lee , has wronged you. Isabel and her sons are going into counsel with him. You can stay with me."

"Oh, o.k. I don't understand all of this, but OK."

"I have an idea, let's you and me go to the waterfall and relax while we wait for them to get finished..."

"Sure, whatever you say..."

Raynar led AlaHandrea to a beautiful, secluded part of the falls area and put up a couple of hammocks. They each had their own, hanging side by side.

The beautiful imposter just smiled to herself thinking about the possibility of making love to that gorgeous watcher... A blind woman could see what he was up to, as far as she was concerned.

As they laid in their hammocks, swaying in the gentle breeze,

Raynar talked to her about space travel and other inhabited planets.

She asked him all kinds of questions about life forms on other worlds.

Then, she surprised him... "Raynar, do you think I'm pretty? Do you find me to be desirable?"

"Oh, sweet, precious girl! You are every man's dream!" Ray told her.

"Oh, thank you for saying that. Say, if I played with you, would you go running off and tell Isabel?"

"Huh? You mean..." He paused, then stood up, helped her to her feet, pulled her close and said, "by play, you mean like this?" Then he kissed her with a bit of passion.

Afterwords, he pinned her wrists, and kissed her more aggressively... "You want me to do things to you, don't you?" He asked her as he held her where she couldn't get away. "Admit it, you want me to just take what I want, as long as I satisfy you in the process... "

He pinned her wrists behind her back and exposed her breasts. Her breathing indicated it was turning her on.

I want to look at you! All of you! You've become a very beautiful woman...

Remember me telling you that the day would come when you and I would be together ... but you had to grow up first... well, you grew up!

Wow!

Did you ever grow up!

Of course, I desire you! Show me a male who does not!

How does it feel to know you create desire in every creature...." He asked, then kissed her again... this time, he became very dominating and pushy... gentle, but unrelenting... she'd struggle a little, then he'd show off some skill and the squirming had new meaning...

Raynar redesigned foreplay!

He was an expert in the subject, taking his time... building the heat to new levels of intensity... making the joining feel so incredible there were no words to describe...

During a quick break, AlaHanDrea positioned herself in a hammock, sideways... when Raynar returned, he smiled the naughtiest smile...

He also learned to love hammocks that day......

It was all Raynar could do to keep knowing about the imposter to himself.... Truthfully, he was rather fond of the mimic and wished that he could just come right out and say it...

"Raynar, thank you."

"You're welcome? Thank me, for what?"

"For seeing me, knowing me, then using me to fulfill your fantasy. It was incredible and I loved it!"

"You know I know... You knew from the start... Didn't you? Then, thank You!" He took her in his arms again and kissed her with honest emotions... He kissed her, not the image she portrayed... She kissed him back with all the love she felt in her heart...

"Raynar we connected, I can feel you... and I know that you connected to me as much as I connected to you. I love you Raynar, there, I said it. I love you..." A tear rolled down his cheek, he lifted her up to him to kiss her, so, she wrapped her legs around him... They became lost in that kiss as they connected, that time, knowing they both knew each other's true identities... They made love to one another... They consummated the connection they felt for each other.

It's not that he didn't Love Isabel, because he did, a lot happened between them. A whole lot of intense pain happened between them for a very long time..... Her husband came back.

Her other husband.

As much as he didn't want to let it affect him, it did ...

Even though George had Barbara...

What he felt with this beautiful creature, was real, true, deep, special, brand new with no bruises...

It was fresh, honest and beautiful with nobody else involved.

In those moments, he cared more about how the lady he was with was feeling and going to feel, then he worried about the woman he was leaving at home.

His concern was, to not hurt the one he was holding in his arms.

What truly mattered to him, was what had been created between the two of them... It was nothing short of magical, but even more than that. They belonged to one another... No ceremonies, or somebody telling them it was okay...

They belonged to one another because they just did ... it was natural ...they came together like two pieces of a puzzle, fitting together... so perfectly... And you just don't damage something like that...

"So, what's the deal with baby girl?" Raynar asked, as they lay snuggled up, in the hammock.

"You know I love her, or I wouldn't be here.

You know my kind.

You know we choose someone that we would like to be.

After observing her for a very long time, I could already see what was going to happen when she began to develop into a woman.

I chose to take her most difficult years from her.

She is safe and protected, where she will remain until she's of an age that men won't just destroy her self image.

Creatures are selfish.

I don't care what your species is.

Y'all don't care what it does to her, y'all just see what you want & you take it.

I'm only glad that someone took the initiative to finally educate males, so that at least, the females get to enjoy it!

Males can be totally heartless! You can't deny that!

I do realize, that there are a lot of females that can also be heartless. So, let's just say, creatures are heartless and selfish beings.

The best gift that I could give her for her birthday, was to relieve her of the worst years of her life! and I've taken it for her and I got to tell you, it's not pretty!

Actually it stinks to high heavens.

I thank God that she doesn't have to truly experience this!

She is safe.

We should go see her, though, it's been a while, since I've been back.

She will be happy to see you."

All we told her, was there was a terrible disease that was felt worldwide... and ... that was not a total lie!

The teenage years are nothing less than insanity!

And ...

that's a disease...

Insanity is a disease...

So, I only sorta lied to her...

Well, not really lied so much... more like implied."

"You really must love that girl to protect her from being a teenager... But sweetie, the teen years..."

"Let me stop you right there! We are not talking about the average creature here!

We are talking about AlaHanDrea!"

"Now, that's true, you're right.

Ok, I won't out you unless I have to, and we will go see baby girl.

She will understand as well as appreciate it.

She will want to watch on screen!"

"You really think she would?"

"I really know she would... I really think she should...

No, that would be torture. Later, when she's a little older, I will give her the memories back."

"I can see how that would be possible and probable.

This is your area of expertise, so I'll leave you alone with the details and respect and honor what you say.

I can't disagree with you. Not when you're right.

Isabel already knows."

"You love Isabel."

"I do.

I love you.

I connected with you...

There's no denying it and I will not be without you."

I will not do a thing to hurt you......

I love you.

You're part of me now.

You just are."

Chapter 3

Isabel froze in her tracks, as images flooded her mind.

She knew in that moment that she had just lost Raynar.

He allowed another women to fill his heart, left empty when he returned from that mission and heard that his wife was living with her first husband and children.

She had tried to get back into his heart, but his walls were thick from grief.

Sadness sunk in and filled ever inch of her... Making her sit down where she stood and shift back to Dragon state... Slowly returning to her lair... Head hung low.

She felt him fall in love with another...

She had so badly wanted that to be her ...

The grieving woman dragon had a 'screw the world's' attitude.

If anyone even attempted to get near her lair, she'd blow an inferno at them....

She clearly did not want to be disturbed...

By anyone...

Raynar felt her grief ...

"There's someone else we've got to go see, right now ... Isabel..."

"See? See how you are? I play with you and you run straight to Isabel!" She teased, trying to make light of the situation...

"You're right, Baby, she deserves respect.

I didn't know it was going to happen.

I didn't mean to take her man from her."

Raynar kissed her on top of her head.

"I'm sorry to get you involved. I didn't think about any of this when I was busy connecting with you, you're a gorgeous beautiful creature...... You, not the image you portray, but you... the one I see... The one I truly see... Of course we belong together... We just do ..."

"Raynar!" George called out.

"George, I can explain..."

"I wish I could kill you, Raynar!" George's eyes were red with fire!

"George, ..." George interrupted him, "what's the matter with you? And with baby girl???"

"George! That's not AlaHanDrea!" Raynar protested.

"What do you mean, it's not AlaHanDrea? I have eyes!"

"And your eyes do not tell you the truth! This creature is not AlaHanDrea! Baby girl is safe and sound and still a virgin! She has been replaced by a mimic!"

"What?!"

"You heard me. And George, I didn't mean for it to happen! But, you, of all people/dragons, should understand!

Her and I connected!

We just did! I was doing the same thing you did, fulfilling a fantasy... But we connected..."

"Are you separating from Isabel?"

"No. I will not abandon my, our Isabel! I don't know what to do, George!"

"So, our family just grew... ?"

"Ya, I think it did...?"

"Isabel!" They both called out, not daring to go near her cave.

"What? What... Do ... You ... Want?"

"Now Isabel, please calm down and try to understand... Please accept this creature into our lives... " Raynar pleaded.

"And what of baby girl? Where is AlaHanDrea?

Where is our baby girl, Raynar?"

"She is safe. There are other questions at hand. For instance, Brad Lee stole what he believed were AlaHanDrea's eggs!

Those children are mimics! Dragon mimics! And they are not his only... He stole them! He drugged her and stole them! Then hid them out... He left her laying in the dirt!

Drugged!

Vulnerable!

It's a great thing that Danalli found her... Only Danalli drugged her and threw her in a cage!"

"Oh, this is just too much!" George said.

"Really? You had sex with her believing it Was baby girl!" Raynar snapped.

"Now, boys!" Isabel chastised. "He's right, tho, George. You did do that."

Barbara walked in, "excuse me, who did what to whom? George!"

"Uh, now Barbara, uh..."

"Don't you now Barbara me!"

The mimic walked over to George, looked him in the eyes and became George. Then, he walked over to Barbara and kissed her with love... Left her starry eyed. Then looked like her.

Isabel spoke up first, "oh what a lovely and fun addition to our family!!! Have you a name?"

"Mimi."

"Cute."

"I can fulfill your every fantasy..."

"Mimi, I think we shall enjoy having you as a part of us," Barbara commented.

"So let me get this straight, I get to love all of you and it's okay?" Mimi asked.

"Yes. In a nutshell, yes."

"So I have two husbands and two wives."

"Yes."

"Hmmm, okay, cool. But we are uneven, so who do I get to sleep with? I connected with Ray... So, do I sleep on one side of Ray and Isabel you sleep on the other?"

"Well yeah, unless well, unless George is laying down with Isabel and then I suppose Barbara will be on one side of Ray and you on the other?"

"So, Barbara belongs to Ray and to George."

Ray smiled a big smile, a mischievous smile, walked over to Barbara bent her backwards and gave her the biggest kiss... made her knees go weak!

"Okay it's time to test this theory... George and Isabel need some time together anyway... I've been monopolizing George... Everyone's been very patient with me and I appreciate it. And I do believe the time has come... yes, the time has come. " Barbara said to the group.

The smile on Raynar's face was priceless to see.

Mimi spoke up, "I think I'm making out pretty good here. I've got king of the world, Queen of the world, Crown Prince in line for the throne of the Watchers, and a very beautiful human. I should say that I'm making out pretty good in this deal!"

Barbara spoke up, " so Mimi, are you male or female?"

"That's a very good question Barbara. I'm whatever you want me to be. We have no gender. We are neither, yet we are both.

We reproduce on our own, requiring no mate for such things.

We are what we choose to be and we can be anything we want to be, anyone we want to be. And yes, I lay eggs and I can be made to lay eggs by a male, and I can cause a female to lay eggs. I can impregnate a female, such as a human, provided I look like a male at the time I'm with her. I can reproduce with just about anything. However I cannot become pregnant, because I do not have a uterus, ever, thank God.

Those are my babies he stole. Brad Lee stole my babies! He drugged me, knocked me out, and stole my babies, then left me in the dirt at the mercy of whoever and whatever found me!

In Danalli's defense, I believe, he was attempting to protect me, AlaHanDrea. "

"Wait, what? What about my son and AlaHanDrea?" Barbara asked. Then added, "so, you're neither, yet both..."

"Correct I believe it's time for all of us to go see baby girl." Mimi told everyone. A moment later, they were all standing on a beach. Mimi looked like Braynar. Everyone looked at him surprised. "Ok so I've been him once or twice...."

AlaHanDrea saw them standing on the beach ... she couldn't believe her eyes!

She ran as fast as she could ....stopped just before getting to them... Then fell to her knees... Crying...

They all rushed over to her. Braynar scooped her up in his strong arms, cradling her like a baby. Then set her down, hugging her... Isabel pulled her away from Mimi and hugged her close.

"I can't believe you are all here! You found me! Y'all are Alive!"

"Yes, sweet girl, we all survived it, each in our own time. Are you o.k baby girl?"

"Yes, I think I am. Are you here to take me home?"

"Baby girl, you are infected. That's Why you are here. You're not over it yet. It takes years to get past this infliction."

"Are you not afraid to catch it from me?"

"Oh, heavens no. We can't catch it from you. We've already been through it."

"Then, why can't I come home?"

"Because it's dangerous for you."

"Well, may I please take a walk with Braynar?"

Braynar took her by the hand and led her down the Beach.

"I'm not sure we are doing the right thing." Isabel said.

"But, if she were living her own life, she would be the mother of stolen children!" Barbara said.

"We don't know that! Baby girl would not have made the same choices as the mimic has made. The mimic wants to experience everything... AlaHanDrea would have shown restraint. At least, I like to think she would have."

"Listen up, for one thing, y'all seem to have lost sight of the fact that we are all now in grave danger! We are on Mimic island! Let that sink in for a moment! We rule the fricking world and just placed ourselves at the mercy of mimics... we have no guarantee that AlaHanDrea will still be the real deal once they return! We need to leave... right now!" George said, quietly. Everyone held hands and Raynar took them all home... or, at least, he thought he did.

He grabbed ahold of Barbara and demanded she be bound and held...

"Mimics traded her out right in front of our faces!" she screamed for help, so, Isabel quietened her. Raynar was right, she Was a mimic!

George and Raynar stared at each other for a good little bit before being certain they were both authentic. Isabel was placed in a cell, but only for a short time before they were certain she had been switched! Both ladies were bound... unable to use their magic...

"George, I do believe we are about to be invaded! Look, there's some plants that will help us, call the guards. Have them round up all of the milk thistle they can find and bring it to us asap. It's deadly poison to mimics. They will not be able to tolerate the sight of it! Next, we need to rescue the ladies."

"You felt them, didn't you, Raynar?" George commented.

"I'm a watcher, George. It's my job. Taking us to see Baby Girl was a ruse to capture us. I'm calling my brothers and my father!"

"Great idea!"

"RAYNAR, BRO, YOU DID the right thing, calling us like you did. Ya know, there's a reason those creatures live on an isolated island! They are extremely dangerous! Our father needs to handle this one!" Healix told them.

Jax objected! "Throw our father in danger? Have you lost your mind?"

"Well, who then, bro?" Healix asked.

"O.k., let's call dad!"

"Better yet, let's go see dad!"

"Wait, brothers, here, hold this please..." Raynar handed milk thistle to them and they both took it without hesitation.

Raynar produced a viewing screen and called their father instead.

3 minutes later, Isabel, Barbara and AlaHanDrea stood in front of the men.

"It's why I'm the king, sons!" Was all their father had to say. "Dad, wait!" Raynar called out.

"What?"

"What about the mimics?"

"Security has been heightened."

A sadness filled Raynar as the reality began to set in... he vanished....

"He will recover. What he suffers from is reality. A fractured dream. It was not ever real. It won't be easy for him, but he is strong and will recover. For now, leave him be. All of you! I will tend to my boy..." the screen went dark.

No one knew quite what to say! George had 2 women to console. AlaHanDrea became ill.

Healix called his dad back and described her symptoms... "son, she is feeling your brothers grief, through Jax. She connected herself to y'all when she was absorbing Jax. She will suffer for as long as he suffers. That gives me an idea! If she feels him, then he feels her! We need to throw a welcome home party for her! Pull out all of the stops, appeal to her gigantic ego! Tantalize the teenager in her! Go for broke! Use her to heal Raynar! it's not a suggestion!!! "

"Yes, your majesty!" They all said in unison.

"And look here! The girl is a woman! Stop at NOTHING!"

"As you wish!"

Chapter 4

Word of AlaHanDrea and the Mimic spread faster than juicy gossip at the beauty shop!

It seemed every broadcast channel on Taurus 9 was carrying the story of the imitation teen queen.

Before the story broke, humanity wasn't aware of mimic island, nor did they seem to be aware of the extreme danger of mimics...

Many thought that dragon kind was being too harsh on the creatures.

Ignorance can be a very bad thing ..

Leon couldn't believe his ears!

How had he missed that? It HAD to have been after ... unless... it was the mimic he was seeing! Yes, that HAD to be it!

He'd seen the mimic and not her! But one thing he knew for certain, he was in love with AlaHanDrea, no matter what her natural form was!

He loved her, plain and simple. The upside to a creature such as her, was that she could put herself in a desirable form... she could make herself so beautiful to look at! A definite upside....

____

AlaHanDrea was so glad to be back home!

"So, I was being saved from being a teenager?"

"That's what the mimic said," Jax told her.

"Do you not believe it? Does the mimic lie?"

"I don't think the mimic lies. They don't usually lie. It's just not in their make up to do so.

But, my dad doesn't trust them!

He must have a good reason!

But then, logic tells me not to trust them!

They are extremely dangerous creatures! Whether or not they mean to be, they are."

"Ya, I can understand that. I'm sure the mimic meant no harm to me, but I really appreciate being able to live my own life and not have somebody step in and live parts of it for me. It was a nice gesture, however... how can I grow if I don't live it myself?" AlaHanDrea commented...

"I have to tell you, she, it, spared you some unpleasantness, for sure.

There are creatures who have brought shame to themselves behind your teenage years. They will be dealt with."

"Such as?"

"OK I guess I should start with the most urgent situation at hand. Brad Lee..."

"Brad Lee?" I used to have such a crush on him!

"Ya, well, he drugged the mimic, stole her eggs and left her laying unconscious in the dirt outside of a small cave. Fortunately, Danalli found it, thinking it was you, drugged it and put it in a cage in his secret lair..."

"WHAT??? You're kidding, right?"

"I wish I were. Also, there's an alien creature, a werewolf, that fell very much in love with you... uh, the mimic...."

"Oh boy.... What's a werewolf?" She asked, feeling confused.

"Well, I'm not real sure. He was born a human, but became a werewolf. I dunno, some kind of human wolf... Not simply a shape shifter, a human wolf. Or, something like that. He's certainly a vicious warrior and predictor... Or, a vicious predator that makes a great warrior."

"Oh... O.K... ?"

"AlaHanDrea, the mimic was very sexually active, looking like you."

"Oh great! And here I am, still a virgin..."

"Here you are, 18 years old and still a virgin!" He repeated...

"Please send a thank you gift to my mimic..."

"As you wish."

"If they fell in love with her, then, chances are, she too, fell in love... oh, that poor baby!"

"My poor brother... Raynar is why you feel so badly." Jax finished explaining things to AlaHanDrea.

"Raynar..... Hmmmm... Wait, what? George??? And he thought it was ME? O.K. O.K. Well, now...

O.k.

Jax, the solution is a simple one. Send Raynar to mimic island. When it's time for him to leave, make him pass through milk thistle... allow him the ability to come and go at mimic island. That serves 2 purposes ... or more... "

A viewing screen popped up, much to their surprise... "young lady, you amaze me! Your wisdom is unmeasurable. Add me to the list of beings that love you! And, I mean that! Child, you are in my heart!" The king of the watchers told her.

Moments later, she felt the grief dissipate...

Jax was getting them some drinks.

" I love you, too, your majesty..." she said out loud, hoping he heard her...

A message arrived for the watcher king. "Your majesty, I love you, too. I have loved you even before I was born.. this Time... I also have a bit of a question for you.

I have come of age. My virginity is a valuable asset.

Maybe too valuable. Please correct me if I'm wrong here, but would my virginity not belong to you?

Is it not yours to harvest?"

AlaHanDrea suddenly vanished.

A viewing screen reappeared... "AlaHanDrea's homecoming party is postponed for three days..." then it vanished.

Since she had asked her question by messenger, Jax had no idea what was going on, he just knew that his father was involved.

Jax hurried to spread the news that her welcome home would happen when she returned home! She had suddenly been called away, but should return in a few days.... As confusing as it was...

"Hello, your majesty, it's good to once again be in your company." AlaHanDrea said to the watcher king.

"You offer me your virginity..."

"I offer you what is rightfully yours to take! How and who would I ever choose to be my first??? Please, tell me that? Are you not entitled to the things with the most value?????? Please tell me then, what holds more value than my virginity? If my virginity was offered, a stampede would occur!"

"You do have some very good points... however, we can't just get naked and do the deed."

"Nor did I suggest that!"

"True!"

"Question, if I was on my wedding night, I would already know that my night was going to include sex, would I not?"

"That's true." He reached over and grabbed her, pulling her into his arms, then gazed into her eyes... kissing her with passion. "I see you! I know who you are! Were...! I see you! I don't know if I can do this. Not and let you go again. I lost you once already." then he kissed her again, she kissed him back.

"Yes, you can do this. You will hate yourself if you do not! You will always regret it! I don't mean to remember that far back, I really don't! But, I do. Well, I do a little bit. Enough. Enough to know that I meant the world to you once. Enough to know that in your mercy, you will help me to forget the past... before now... I never want to forget what we are about to enjoy."

"Are you certain this is what you want?"

Wasn't it you that said so many times that you'd give anything to be able to hold me one more time? To make love to me one more time? Well, this is your one more time... I never want to forget meaning the world to you. Not unless it begins to interfere in my now life..."

AlaHanDrea dropped her top, exposing her breasts... he just sat, staring at her, so, she dropped her skirt... wrapped her arms around his neck and kissed him with love and passion. Then whispered in his ear, "I will always love you!"

Desire took him over! He couldn't help himself! It had been centuries since he had held her in his arms... AlaHanDrea used magic to remove his clothing. He was so forceful! Very aggressive... she couldn't have stopped him if she'd have wanted to!

He stopped himself. " We can't, I can't... It's not fair to either of us. Especially to you... Especially to me... "

He used his magic to put their clothes back on...

It's not fair to my wife and sons ...

I'm not free and truthfully, neither are you!

You are just beginning your life!

You're not free to commit, not yet.

You need to experience life first....

I'm so glad I decided not to destroy you!"

"You we're going to destroy me?"

"The subject did come up, once, a very time ago. But, I chose to send all three of my sons to look after you, instead... just know this, AlaHanDrea, I know you girl! I don't just know who you were, I know who you are this time around! Better than anyone else, except, for God himself, girl, I see you!

I already know about the whole steering currents thing... so don't even try to deny it! I already know... I already know how easily you changed the direction of that galaxy!

I know that you knew it only took a pebble tossed into the creek to change the flow.... I know that you planned on absorbing my son, still, I allowed you to live. Don't do that again... there are other watchers besides MY sons, girl...

I already know you, AlaHanDrea and don't you ever forget it!"

"Yes, sir." Was all she said.

"I'm always here for you." he told her.

When she woke up, she was in her own bed... in her new home...

Jax and Healix were there.... Waiting for her return. Isabel arrived shortly after she woke up.

"Baby girl, the mimics children have been sent to mimic island. Even half mimics are not allowed in our world, they are just too dangerous. We aren't sure what to do about Brad Lee. Since he was certain it was you he was doing all of that to, you have a say as to what happens to him."

"Seriously, Isabel?"

"Seriously.

"Isabel, it's no secret that BradLee is a bad boy! No one has ever accused him of being a Boy Scout. Don't you think that taking his children is pain enough? He obviously wants children. I can understand why he tried to hide them from me. He was afraid he would lose them... I also believe he was watching over me until Danalli found me. Just as I believe that Danalli thought he was protecting me!

I don't, won't, believe that either of them meant for harm to come to me. It's not logical. When in doubt, apply logic.... "

"So, you think that Brad Lee simply wanted children of his own?"

"Yes, I believe that Brad Lee felt himself make eggs with me and didn't want to give them up! I think that Crotchety old dragon wanted babies of his own... since when do we fault a guy for wanting to be a father? Yeah OK, he made some mistakes. He's also paying for those mistakes by losing his children! That's pretty severe punishment, don't you think? Heck, I still want to go out with the guy ... course, I'll be careful with him now that I know what he's capable of. I just feel that he has been punished enough, poor guy. And ...he lost his kids ... And... everybody's talking about him like he's some kind of rapist... from what I'm understanding, it was not rape. From what I understand, the mimic was a loosey-goosey!"

"AlaHanDrea, while she was being you, she responded to electrical stimulation. Sex energized her."

"Sex energizes me? For real? Wow! Good to know! Cool, sex energizes me... good to know... "

"AlaHanDrea, there's something else I seriously need to tell you... about... Dane... he got married... he chose a full time mate... very un-mer like... to choose only one wife... " Isabel told her everything... island and all...

Dane told me he and I were going to grow old together... he told me he loved me and I believed him... he wrote me songs about our love and our lives together...

Isabel instantly regretted telling her, when she saw tears rolling down AlaHanDrea's cheeks... she quietly turned and walked away, to allow the teen queen time to process it all.

"How could Dane do that? " she said out loud to no one.

"We all made mistakes, sweet girl..." Leon said, standing in the doorway.

"Leon? Leon! Oh, Leon!"

She ran into his arms and hugged him tightly.

They both sat down beside each other.

"AlaHanDrea, how old were you when you got switched?"

" 12. And it took my mom. Told me they had a body for her to move into."

"Oh, baby girl!" he took her in his arms and held her close. For a moment.

"You're 18."

"I'm 18."

"You're 18."

He looked deeply into her eyes, innocence looked back at him. He tilted her face up with his finger on her chin and kissed her so sweetly, then with more passion as Sparks flew!

She melted in his arms. Heat began to rise as he kissed her neck, then her lips again... It was all he could do to stop himself!

In a moment of weakness, he picked her up, carried her over to her bed and laid her down, crawling in beside her...

"I have to stop. Please, tell me to stop."

"I can't do that!"

"Why not?"

"Because! I don't want you to stop! Leon, I don't want you to stop! I love you, Leon!"

"AlaHanDrea, I'm afraid I'm going to have to be the grown up here and force myself to...." She interrupted him with a kiss...

"Woman, now... That's so not fair! I love you so much! However, we just can't. You just can't! I don't care who the male is! That mimic gave you a gift! You reached 18 in tact! Let's keep you that way.

Baby girl, I did something with the mimic I'm now going to do for you... Because I love you and because you need this!

Oh boy, o.k.... baby girl... I'll be right back...."

Leon was only gone for a moment. " I need you to put this on. You won't be able to take it off until it's time for it to come off."

"What is it?"

"A pregnancy simulator."

"Seriously Leon?"

"Very..."

She looked deeply into his eyes, then reluctantly, agreed.

She slipped the vest on and heard it lock.

He didn't mention the fact that it contained a Chasity strap!

"So, tell me, what was life like on mimic island?" Leon asked her.

She told him all about her years in isolation ..

"Baby girl, you've been through a lot. You've been traumatized.

Please don't allow trauma, hormones and the like, to be responsible for you giving up something as precious as your virginity.

None of us are going anywhere.

You need time to choose correctly.

This is not something to be rushed into.

Yes, I do want you! Of course I want you! Woman, you drive me wild! However, I also love you very much. Too much to take advantage of you!"

Chapter 5

"Your majesty, Queen Isabel, there's a man? Here, insisting on an audience with you. He says it's urgent. Queen Isabel, he claims to be AlaHanDrea's ...... Father!"

Jason of the royal guard said to the distracted queen.

"Do what?!?!?

O.K... bring him to me at once!

Go!

Now!"

"Yes, my queen!"

Moments later, Jason returned with the strangest looking little fella.

Isabel could not even begin to guess his species...

"This is the one claiming to have sired AlaHanDrea?" Isabel asked, in disbelief...

"Your majesty, my name is Jeffry. Ion 6 was where I was created.

My loves name is Folica. Folica and I are that girls rightful parents, I just know that we are! And your majesty, I do love Folica! She refused to listen to me when I tried to talk to her. She made it clear to me that she never wanted to see me again, so, I left her alone.

Then, we got moved. I heard Folica was dead and heard nothing of the child. Then I was moved

But, after seeing those videos being broadcast... Well, queen Isabel, that's my baby girl!"

Isabel stared him in the eyes for the longest time, neither one blinked ...

"I will discuss this with my husband's and wife. In the mean time, you will remain here. Guards, lock him in Chambers. At once!"

"Yes, your majesty."

"Wait, Jeffry, Folica lives. Jason, retrieve Folica and put her in chamber with Jeffry. Please inform her that she is to listen to what he has to say. And she is to listen with both ears and hear him! And Jeffrey, she wears a new body. Your child saved her spirit and carried her spirit with her until a body became available. I hope you two can work things out...

Take him..."

"George! Raynar! Barbara! Jax! Healix! King Leon! King Bjorn! King William! King Peaorin! King Bronah!

They all arrived, looking bewildered over the group she had summoned.

Isabel filled the men in, repeating what Jeffry had told her...

"We can't keep this from her..." King Bjorn commented.

"Ya, but she's just returned home after being missing for years! " Jax told them.

"The dudes timing could not be worse!" Bronah commented. "Surely that wasn't the first video he has seen of her! Baby girl is 18 years old! Why does he come forward now?"

"I say we wait a minute. Keep him here... Uh... Uh oh... O.K. I just received a message from my father... Jeffry is AlaHanDrea's father.

He was put in the transport tunnels on my father's orders... According to my father, lives are easier taken than restored... " Healix told the group .

"I say we keep him here and try to find out why he has waited so long to attempt to stake a claim. We can always tell her, but we cannot un-tell her..." William added.

"I don't want to tell her at all. I think her parents should tell her themselves." Bjorn said.

Isabel spoke up... "When the time is right, I will tell her! Bronah, may I have a word with you please?"

"About Braynar and the girls?"

"You're a good guesser!"

"Uh oh, what happened with Braynar and the fairies?" William asked.

Isabel filled everyone in on the details of the attack. The bears, lions and wolves had no idea that fairies were so dangerous! They excused themselves and rushed back to their own kinds to educate their citizens...

Raynar walked over to Isabel, took ahold of her elbow and quietly walked her into her chamber, closing the door behind him.

"Woman, I have loved you since high school!

The kind of love I have for you has no equal and cannot be replaced.

What I felt, feel, or thought I felt for the mimic cannot be compared in any way to my feelings for you!

I'm so sorry that I hurt you! It was not ever my intention! I can stand here and make excuses all day long... But there's never a good excuse for hurting you! I was wrong and I deeply regret having done so.

I'm so tired of others being involved in us... No, I do not want to change our family.

You need to spend some George time.

I want to spend some Barbara time!

Not just in the sack... I want to get to know Barbara... You and George need to take a vacation and revisit the subject of more children.

Neither of you have dealt with the loss of your last eggs.

Until you do, it will remain an obstacle between the 4 of us.

Please, you and George leave here, today, go to the islands. Put the boys in charge and just go! When you get back, we can deal with Baby girls parents and the rest of the planets issues."

"Raynar... I love you!"

"I love you, too. Now, go! Right now! Go grab George and just go! Come back with eggs!"

Isabel took off outta her Chambers, grabbed George and they were gone. Raynar went over to Barbara.

"Pretty lady, don't fret. Those two have stuff to take care of that doesn't really involve you and I.

I requested this time alone with you. All of this is my idea, my doing..."

Raynar told Barbara.

"You requested time alone with me?"

"Woman, I'm as much your husband as George is, so ya, I requested this time for you and I. Don't you think we need it? Do you not think we deserve it?"

Barbara didn't quite know what to say!

"Barbara, dark is coming soon," he took her hands in his and pulled her close, then kissed her softly on the lips, causing sparks to fly. So, he kissed her with a bit of passion, taking her breath away!

The sound of the rhythm drums beginning filled the early evening air.

Raynar could tell that Barbara didn't want him to stop. He dipped her and kissed her with deep passion , igniting a fire deep within them both.

"There is not one thing wrong with you and I... You are my wife! I am your husband! I would like to be the father of your child..." Raynar told her, then kissed her again. She melted in his arms...

Raynar had intended to wait until after they had spent some time together, but desire interfered with that plan!

He scooped her up in his arms and carried her into her chamber and locked the door.

"You are so beautiful! So, very beautiful... I can see why George fell in love with you!

I can see why I'm falling so deeply in love with you…!"

"You're falling in love with me?"

"Have you no feelings for me?"

"Oh Raynar, yes, yes I have feelings for you! Of course I do! I've tried to hold back, uncertain of what's acceptable .."

"You're my wife! I'm your husband! We're married, Barbara!"

She smiled real big, grabbed the front of his shirt and pulled him to her and they both fell backwards, landing on the bed, laughing… He gazed into her eyes and said, "let's make a baby…" Then kissed her again…

Evening parties were in full swing when Raynar and Barbara finally went out looking to see where they were going to spend the evening.

The first thing Raynar did was to sing a song to Barbara. He hadn't told her yet that he felt himself give her a baby, but he said it in the songs he sang, hoping she'd catch on… his songs spoke of how their baby would unite Braynar and Danalli for centuries to come.

They danced together, sang together… Laughed together… Then went home and slept together.

The next morning, Raynar took her out to play with her magic and discovered more of the things she inherited from baby girl.

Barbara and Raynar both got to know Barbara better… The new Barbara…

After the experience with the mimic, Raynar realized that he had enough women in his life, decided his time would be better spent enjoying the 2 he already had. After all, what more could any man want than what he already had?

All he had managed to do, chasing dreams, was to hurt everyone involved, when there was plenty of everything at home.

Chapter 10 B

Chapter 6

"Keithen!" AlaHanDrea squealed, ruining into his arms for a hug. "Keithen! Look at you! You're a man! Wow! And What a man you are!"

Keithen smiled at her, relieved she knew nothing of the teen years with the mimic...

His smile made her tingle all over...

He stood in front of her, gazing into her eyes...

When his lips touched hers, Sparks flew!

He took her breath away!

"Wow! Keithen!" She giggled...

Then took a step back.

"AlaHanDrea, I love you! I've always loved you. You're a woman now. I can show you just how much I love you," Keithen kissed her with heat and passion.

After the kiss, she took another step back. Keithen took her hands in his. She gripped his hands tightly, then let go and pulled back.

"Oh... Keithen.... Seriously, Keithen?

I see it all...

You say You love me? Don't you mean to say, you love me still being a virgin? You love me not knowing what you did with the mimic? You love my innocence and an opportunity to pick my flower? I have one question for you, have you no shame?

You're supposed to be one of my best friends... and this is what I can expect from you?

You may look like a man, but from here, it looks to me like you have some major growing up to do, man!

You will not hurt me to gain your pleasure!

I'll not allow it!

You think I can't see you? You think I wouldn't know?

Or find out?

What did you plan to do once I found out?

You thought you were going to take advantage of my not knowing and pick my flower?

Not caring how'd I feel once I learned the truth?

Apparently, you have no concept for my power!

If you did, you would have never believed the mimic was me!

You can't lie to me and you can't hide the truth from me either!

Who do you think you are?

You may be heir to the throne of Drakonia, but I, am Queen Ala Han Drea!

Maybe you've been too close to me to properly appreciate who and what I am!

Maybe it's time you get it through your head who it is you stand before!

You met me as a young child, but make no mistake, you met greatness when you met me!!!

You will NOT pick my flower!" She slapped the shit out of him, leaving a hand print on his cheek... then vanished.

"Wow! Bro! I heard that! Ouch!" Braynar said as he walked over to Keithen. " Looks like she's not the push over you thought she was..."

"Danalli!" AlaHanDrea squealed...

"Well.... There's my baby girl..."

AlaHanDrea ran up to Danalli, wrapped her arms around his neck and gave him a big hug. Her feet were dangling in the air, so she wrapped her legs around his waist and kissed him all over his face, then hugged him again.

"Well, hello to you, too..." He teased. He thought better of moving in for a romantic kiss ...

She moved around to his back, piggy back...just like she did as a child ... Often times, she'd sit on the side of his hip as well as piggy back. She loved being playful with Danalli.

She just wanted to be close to him. Sitting on his back leaning over his shoulder, was intimate without being romantic.

He'd always allowed her to snuggle him in that 'safe manner'.

There was nothing inappropriate about sitting on his back...

AlaHanDrea was small when compared to her closest friend. AlaHanDrea was small when compared to a lot of creatures, only measuring about 5'7"...

And she loved climbing on him... doing acrobatic stunts and such... Especially when he was in dragon state.

When they were both feeling playful, she do a one handed hand stand, holding one of his hands! Then, she'd do the splits while balancing on his hand... He's toss her into the air where she'd do flips and such before he'd catch her again... They'd do a huge variety of stunts, just having fun...

Danalli shifted for her and took to the skies, with her riding on his neck......

AlaHanDrea was really enjoying their fly about... It was right what she needed at that moment...

Suddenly, Danalli spotted poachers! A moment later, AlaHanDrea spotted them as well, throwing shields up around her and Danalli both, while her mighty dragon quietly soared towards the ground....

Danalli swooped in and snatched up one of the hunters in his talons before they knew he was there! AlaHanDrea also grabbed one before they regained altitude. She ate hers right away, Danalli waited until he landed.

The hungry dragon questioned the poacher before enjoying the meal he'd just acquired.

"Well, girl, seems there's 5 more! Shall we?"

"Sure! I went a big long time without good protein! And I'm HUNGRY!

Danalli, the others have seen us, shift for me and lets go play with them a little first...

Let's go pretend to be running from the scary dragon!"

"Sound like fun to me!" He agreed, with a chuckle.

AlaHanDrea changed her cloths to barely there, torn and raggedy pieces of fabric that left little to the imagination... both of their clothes appeared as tho they had been n quite some battle!

They began running through the wilderness, as tho escaping with their lives, until they ran across the rest of the poachers...

AlaHanDrea almost lost control when she looked in the poachers cages and saw her Centaurs!

She managed to magically unlock the cages without being noticed.

The poachers were taken with her beauty ... Their eyes bulged when they saw her nearly nude body...... and they had evil on their minds...

Several of the hunters jumped on Danalli, he allowed them to think they had a hold on him, trying his best not to crack up laughing at them.

They had no idea Danalli was a Dragon!

A couple of the other hunters approached AlaHanDrea. She started acting all willing....

"Well, y'all are handsome! Ya know, I'm really tired of being a virgin!" She teased. " Y'all look like you could be all kinds of fun!"

The hunters got all excited when she said that. "Hey, someone pour me some nectar wine and let's get this party started!"

The poachers were tripping over themselves to get alcohol for her.

"Now, make sure y'all have him restrained. It's his job to make sure I remain a virgin...."

""He's not going anywhere, pretty lady..."

"Great! Someone start playing drums, come on with some music, I want to dance! It's time to get rid of this virgin affliction! More wine, please! I want y'all to watch me dance, then I want to taste every one of you!" She teased ...

"Y'all heard the lady! More wine!"

All 5 men began playing drums while AlaHanDrea began dancing around. While all eyes were on her, the Centaurs quietly stepped out of the cages and Danalli easily busted out of his restraints, shifting back to Dragon state.

The poachers were surrounded before they knew it.

AlaHanDrea began dancing in front of one of the men, very seductively, then turned him to vapor and inhaled him right in front of the other men!

The hunters froze as they began to realize the situation they were in...

The Centaurs laughed as AlaHanDrea ate her fill.

She burped and said, "Scuse me!" Then giggled, as usual...

Danalli and the Centaurs laughed with her....

"How were those humans able to imprison Centaurs?" She asked.

"They have developed magic binding weapons," Crole, the oldest of the Centaurs in their group, explained to her.

"O.k. I don't like that one bit. We need to do something about that. I can see now we need to have a talk with George. Be assured my friends, that will happen very soon! We'll put an end to this!

And tell me, since when do the humans come into the wilderness hunting and poaching as if it's okay?

Maybe Dragon kind needs to start doing more flies for food on the mainland!"

"Baby girl, it's always been a problem. Ever since I can remember, it's been a problem. And I agree with you, it's a problem that needs to be solved." Danalli commented.

"Danalli, where is Athena?"

"She's probably working over at the resort ...oh, that's right! you don't know about the resort!

King Neptune built an incredible resort, using the transport tunnel technology under the sea, to allow drylanders the opportunity to go below and get to know the MERS in their natural habitat."

"Seriously?"

"Yes, ma'am!"

Crole spoke up, " us centaurs love going down in the tunnels and being able to be under the sea like that ... that is really cool... We know it wasn't really made for us, but we love it anyway...

Thank you for setting us free! Hopefully we'll see you around real soon ... maybe at the parties tonight?"

"Sure! Stay safe my friends!"

Crole and his brothers ran off back into the wilderness....

"Lots of changes in my absence..."

"Ya, I suppose there were."

"Danalli, when you put who you thought was me, in that cage, were you trying to protect me? I mean, you found me passed out in the dirt, then basically kidnapped me and hid me out... What's the deal?"

"I was tired of watching the abuse and disrespect. I wanted it to stop! So did the fake you... The fake you was already hiding ...

Her feelings had been deeply hurt by those that meant the most to her.

I have to tell you the truth, I'm guilty of having had sex with the fake you, too.

And no, I didn't know she was an imposter." He put himself back in man state, put his arms around her and held her for a moment, kissed her on top of her head, then let her go.

They sat down in a hammock, side by side.

"I'm so sorry, Danalli. I know you would never hurt me. We were dead together, you and I... We've been waiting patiently for me to come of age and here I am, years past coming of age... Everything you thought we were experiencing, never happened for me.

Well, it looks like you get a do over..."

She teased....

"I guess I do, at that! Hey, do you know about Bob?"

He could tell from the look on her face that she wasn't really clear on what he meant. "No worries, there's time for all of that later..."

"Danalli, are You going to pick my flower?"

Danalli almost choked! He coughed a couple of times... AlaHanDrea stood up and stood in front of him...

His heart skipped a beat...

"Well? Are you?"

"Yes Ma'am, I sure am...

I've been waiting a very long time ... But... Not today, I'm not. You're not ready."

"Danalli, I'm so far past ready!"

"Nope. No, you're not. How long have you got to keep that contraption on?"

"It's growing."

"I can see that. Leon's a smart fella!"

"If you say so."

"I say so. He's very wise!

I suppose a more truthful answer to your question would be... I hope it's me that picks that flower. I'm sure it will be either Braynar, Leon or myself, given we are the leading experts in Virgin detail.

But sweetheart, you are Not ready.

Your hormones say that you are, but they don't get a vote!

Woman, you have no idea how hard it is for me right now, c'mon, we need to go ..."

"Danalli, please... Kiss me the way a man kisses a woman.... "

Danalli stood up, kissed her softly, then pulled back. " We are playing with fire, let's go."

"Danalli, please...."

He took her in his arms and kissed her with passion. Desire began building in both of them. Just as Danalli was about to rip that pregnancy vest right off of her, he gained control of himself... Shifted and put her on his back, taking to the air, headed for home.

Isabel was on her way to see AlaHanDrea when they landed.

"Isabel, please make a decree that AlaHanDrea is to have a chaperone at All times... Beginning now!

You may want to make sure the chaperone has a chaperone!"

"Oh, Danalli!" AlaHanDrea protested.

"This one's hormones are raging and I was almost a bad boy. Now, if I may be excused, I have some mermaids to go visit!" Danalli wasted no time diving into the pool leading out to sea...

"Baby girl, looks like you and I will be spending some time together.

Sweetie, this too shall pass.

The day will come when you thank all of us for this.

Please be patient with us. Our only desire is to protect you from the enemy within..."

"I love you, Isabel!"

Isabel immediately threw her shields up and none too soon! AlaHanDrea tried to cocoon her!

The contrary teen queen had a mischievous grin on her face. Isabel knew right then that the fight had just begun! She began summoning everyone, Leon, Danalli, Braynar... All telepathically.

"I'm sorry Isabel, I really am, but I don't... Need... A... Chaperone!" she said as she walked right through Isabel's shields.

Isabel quickly shifted to dragon state and took to the air. Just as she was attempting to gain altitude, a sound wave from AlaHanDrea screaming, slammed into her, sending her rolling through the air!

Isabel turned and blew an inferno at AlaHandrea, her shields deflecting the flames...

Isabel began sending a distress signal as she attempted to flee...

The royal guard responded almost instantaneously...

They found themselves in a position they didn't think they would see themselves in... poised for battle, Shields up... facing against baby girl!

The flock began arriving to protect their Queen.

Part of the flock stood in front of AlaHanDrea, as if to protect her from their own brethren!

The balance of dragons was about equal between the two queens.

Both sides were facing off...

AlaHanDrea puffed up with pride as a multitude of creatures began arriving, standing with the dragons to protect her from their friends, family and their queen!

George, Raynar, Jax and Healix rushed to the scene!

George took Isabel in his arms while the Watcher brothers placed themselves between the two sides...

Jax spoke up first, "STAND DOWN!!! Everybody, Stand Down!

There will be no battle here today! STAND DOWN!" He shouted, causing the ground to quake.

Danalli rushed back and was appalled at what he saw!

"AlaHanDrea! Baby girl! Come on now, baby, stand down." Danalli pleaded.

AlaHanDrea levitated, threw her arms up and shouted, "I... Am QUEEN ALA HAN DREA!!!"

The ground shook under her words...

The watchers were the only ones that didn't bow down to her.

Danalli levitated himself to eye level with her... "What do you think you are doing, AlaHanDrea?"

"No one is the boss of ME!"

"Oh, o.k. so this is how you want to play it...!"

He grabbed her upper arms pulling her up against him, "fine, fine, have it your way! Stop struggling! You're mine right now! I will do with you as I so please, do I make myself clear, young lady?

Stop your squirming, I'm not letting you go!" He pinned both of her hands behind her back with one of his hands and ripped the vest off with the other hand, still levitating in front of a crowd ... He bent her backwards and kissed her with a bit of force until he felt her begin to respond and melt into his arms.

He scooped her up as tho she were a new bride, carrying her to his lair.

Braynar, JayDe, Kenneth, Jason and Franklon stood guard at the caves opening.

Leon walked over and picked the vest up, shaking his head, then walked over to Braynar.

"Raging hormones..."

"Looks like it," Braynar responded.

"What do you think Danalli is doing with her?" Leon asked.

"I know what he's not doing with her!

If he's doing what I think he's doing, he may need back up...

I'm pretty sure he will need back up ....

Lots and lots of back up!"

Danalli came walking towards the guys, calmly, as tho nothing special was going on.

"She's resting.

I bound her magic for a bit.

A little gift King Neptune gave me!" He said smiling, holding up an amulet.

Leon was still shaking his head, "this is not going to be easy! Ya, we should have known the mimic was a fake! No one can equal super bitch!"

"Gentlemen, I do believe we are in up over our heads! This looks like it's going to be a bumpy ride!" Franklon commented...

Chapter 7

" She's waking up!" JayDe told the guys.

"Ah crap," Danalli responded, then rushed over to her side.

"You tricked me! You used magic to tame me!"

"Now, AlaHanDrea, before you get too terribly upset... Sweetheart... I love you! It was for your own good!"

"Blah blah blah. I'm hungry. You're looking pretty good to me!"

"Now! AlaHanDrea! Stop that. I'll go get you something to eat. Behave yourself, would you?"

He stepped outside of the cave, "O.k. guys, please try to keep an eye on her and I'll be back as quickly as I can be. Franklon, come on, come go with me...

okay, we'll be right back."

The two dragons took to the air in search of food......

Braynar was chatting it up with Craigen, Kenneth, Jason and Keithen, so, JayDe took advantage of the opportunity and slipped in to say hello... since, he had not actually met her, just the mimic.

"Hello, who/what are you?"AlaHanDrea asked.

"Hello, I'm JayDe Blackwolf, I'm a werewolf," he explained.

"Oh! Well, hello there, JayDe, I'm to understand that you're in love with me, or who you thought was me."

"Please pardon me for staring, you're just so beautiful! And yes, I fell in love with your beauty. May I please kiss you, once?"

"Only once? But, what if I like it?

Question, why is there so much hair on your face?"

"Because I'm a werewolf," He explained, then shifted to full man state, minus the abundance of facial hair.

"Oh, that's much better! Wow, you're really handsome! Come, sit beside me. Then you can kiss me, once." She giggled.

He went over to her, took her by the hand, stood her up and kissed her... Then hugged her, and kissed her again...

"Thank you. I had to know."

"Had to know what?"

"If it was her I love, or you."

"Well, did you get an answer?"

"Yes, yes I did. Please forgive me because I know you don't know me, but it's you that I love. I suppose I will have to try to convince you to fall in love with me, now.

It seemed like it was an easy task for the mimic... I'm hoping it's just as easy a task for you."

"Only time will tell, JayDe. Just please know that I'm not opposed to the idea .. I also really enjoyed the kisses..."

The smile on JayDe's face made AlaHanDrea giggle a little.

"Ya know JayDe, I was only 12 when the mimic tricked me into going with it. Since I've been back, I have received more than a few kisses. It seems that the males are happy to see me grown."

"Your stunning beauty, I'm sure, gets the credit. You are remarkable!"

"Thank you. It's strange, you're not afraid of me." She remarked.

"That's funny, I think it's strange that you're not afraid of me!" They both laughed.

"On my home planet, I was a loner. People were terrified of me," JayDe explained.

"Me too!"

"I think it's pretty nice to be treated like I'm just an average creature!"

"Ya, me too. I think I like you, JayDe."

"JayDe, dude, I see you met our teen queen," Braynar said as he walked into the cave.

"Hello, Braynar. It's so good to see you. Braynar, may I please speak to you alone for a minute?" AlaHanDrea asked him.

JayDe left without saying a word.

"What's on your mind, pretty lady?"

"You are. You are what's on my mind.

I believe you've filled out more in my absence.

If you don't mind my saying so, you look simply delicious!"

"Uh, Danalli and Franklon went for food."

"Uh, I don't want to eat you, silly. Not like that, anyway." She teased.

Braynar blushed deep red.

"Braynar, would you like to pick my flower?"

"Excuse me?"

"Oh c'mon, you heard me. Would you like to pick my flower? Because I'd just love it if you would," she told him, trying her best to be alluring.

"Oh, baby girl, if you only knew...

But, baby girl, you did a very bad thing!

You attacked my Mother!

My Mother, AlaHanDrea! Which, is why you are now bound.

You had my brethren facing off against one another!"

"Oh c'mon, Bray, don't be so dramatic. Anyway, I was only going to cocoon her! She wasn't hurt by the waves, I only rolled her through the air a little...

She blew flames at me!

Now, you know good and well that you want to!

I'll bet you even did it with the mimic!"

"I'm so sorry, baby girl, yes, I did do it with the mimic.

I suppose I should be ashamed of myself ..."

"I dunno, maybe. I don't see what the big deal is about being a virgin. If I don't want to be any longer, then it should be up to me, shouldn't it?"

"Well, ya, technically, that's true, however, you're in a high hormone stage and not making rational decisions.

Sex makes babies.

I know, it seems so unfair that something that enjoyable has such huge consequences, but life is not always fair.

Are you ready for a baby?"

"No, I am not ready to be a mother. Absolutely not. I don't want to get pregnant...

I don't want to lay eggs...

I don't want to reproduce. I just want to have sex!"

"Well, that's all fine and good, but sex makes babies.

So, what are you going to do if I give you sex and a baby?"

"Is there no way that you and I can be together without risking making a baby?

I mean, is there absolutely no way to have sex without risking making a baby?

Surely we could do it once or twice and not risk getting pregnant.

I mean, who gets pregnant the first time they have sex?"

"The vast majority of All creatures..."

AlaHanDrea rolled her eyes and sighed in frustration.

"Seriously?"

I wouldn't lie to you, AlaHanDrea."

"I suppose I should say thank you for standing with me against your own mother and brethren..."

"Let me stop you right there, baby girl.

You need to understand something, I did not stand with you against my mother and my brethren!

I stood in front of you, because my brethren will not lift a finger against me! It was the only way I had to stop the situation and not allow that situation to escalate!

Never would I ever side against my own mother!

Do you understand that? If it meant killing you, baby girl, or, die trying, then I would die trying... or you would lay dead on the ground.

She is my MOTHER!"

AlaHanDrea's head hung low as clear thought took over for a moment.

"I'm so sorry, Braynar. Please, tell me that you will forgive me! I feel horrible!

Of course I Love Isabel!

I would never bring harm to her!"

"My Mother, our Queen, blew flames at you, because that's all she's got for defense! And, she knew you already had your shields up! She was trying to get you to stop!!!"

"I don't need a stinking chaperone to make my decisions for me!"

"Apparently, you do!

Fine.

That's just fine, AlaHanDrea, you don't want a chaperone, fine, then you won't have one. You want to throw away your virginity as tho it has no value, then fine, throw it away! I will even do it for you, if that's what you really want! Go ahead, get naked and crawl up on that bed! Well? Go on, what are you waiting for? Crawl on up there!"

"Braynar...."

"No, don't now Braynar, me! And don't you be all crying the blues when you go laying an egg!

I'm a dragon, I can't get you pregnant... And I'll carry the egg in my pouch, but you'll take care of it!

Have you ever even been around a baby dragon???"

"Why are you so angry?"

"Because you are being a spoiled child!

You HIT My Mother!

You had my brethren ready to battle one another for caring more about you than you care about you!

Baby girl, I'm ashamed of you!

You are acting like an ungrateful spoiled brat!!!

You're treating the very ones they care about you the most, like the enemy and I'm ashamed of you!"

Tears were streaming down AlaHanDrea's face, her head hung low.

She shrank herself, stepped out of her restraints, then laid down, curled up in a little ball and cocooned herself.

Braynar plopped down in a chair next to her.

Danalli and Franklon made it back. JayDe, Keithen, Kenneth and Craigen filled them in on the butt chewing Braynar had given her, telling them about her cocooning herself in tiny size.

They all felt very bad for AlaHanDrea. Raging hormones could be a terrible thing.

The biggest problem AlaHanDrea had tho, was a total lack of discipline in her life.

No one ever wanted to tell her no, or get onto her about anything. Discipline is needed to develop self discipline. Even those with good self discipline had a difficult time during times of raging hormones.

They all knew that her teenage years were going to be difficult .. they found themselves wondering if the mimic hadn't been right all along...

The men all got comfortable outside of the caves entrance and just inside. The food wagon had plenty for everyone, so they all just made the best of the situation.

Brethren, feeling bad about the whole ordeal, showed up and made a ground fire. Before long, drummers began filling the air with the soothing sounds of rhythm.... Danalli began the singing. Before long, all of the guards were singing like a men's choir singing together.

The singing drew other instruments and before long, the caves entrance was The place to be for evening entertainment.

All of the merriment woke the dozing Braynar. As tempting as it was to go join in the fun, he wasn't about to leave AlaHanDrea's side.

He saw stirring inside of the cocoon and was hoping the music would coax her to come on out.

Tootsie, Cathey, Trina, Dena, all dragon princesses, along with Queen Isabel, came walking into the cave.

"Well, hello ladies! Mother! Y'all are all looking lovely tonight. What's with all the wrapped boxes? Who are all of those gifts for?"

"Hello Braynar! We're all here to see AlaHanDrea. These are all for her. Don't even ask what's in the boxes, just go on outside and leave the ladies to take care of lady business! Go on now, son," Isabel told him.

"Yes, mother. She's in the cocoon, I'm afraid I was a little hard on her. I'll want to see her as soon as y'all say I can. I need to let her know that I'm not angry at her."

"O.k., so, now, run along... We've got this!" Isabel told him.

Athena came running in. "Got here as fast as I could, hello Isabel, ladies!"

Once they were all through with their greetings, it was time to coax AlaHanDrea out of her cocoon.

"AlaHanDrea, it's Isabel. Tootsie, Cathey Ann and the girls are here with me, Athena is here, too! You need to come on out now. We all have presents for you.

Baby girl, none of us are upset with you. We all love you and we have all felt what you are feeling. We've all been where you are. Now, come on out and say hello to everyone.

AlaHanDrea! Now, you come on out of there before I tear that cocoon open! It's ladies hour! O.k. we are going to count to three, then we are all coming in there after you!" They all giggled, agreeing and coaxing until she finally began to slowly open her cocoon.

Everyone said hello to her and told her to hurry up and grow herself so she could open her presents.... They were solutions to her 'problem'.

She was shy to come out, feeling ashamed and embarrassed by her actions.

"AlaHanDrea, please don't be shy. No one is judging you. We are all ladies here and we all understand perfectly.

We are here to tell you that becoming a mother too soon is no picnic.

Nature is mean! Hormones drive us so we will reproduce. If we are in our logical mind, we won't reproduce! So, hormones drive us crazy!

That's Why we are all here to offer you support, sweet girl, please come out. We all love you very much and it's really hard to party with you hiding ..." Isabel told her.

AlaHanDrea finally slit open the cocoon, stepped out and grew herself. Isabel hugged her and told her she forgave her, then apologized for blowing flames at her.

The teen Queens face lit up when she saw Athena, then a frown replaced the smiles, as thoughts of Dane filtered through.

"Isabel told you about Dane, didn't she? Ok I'm so sorry, AlaHanDrea. Please know that Dane Truly loves you." Athena was trying to be convincing.

"While I was in my cocoon, I looked to see what happened with Dane while I was away.

No one can keep secrets from me, ya know.

Athena, Dane came to me, well, the mimic me, and took my virginity, then, erased the memories of it. He came to me more than once, then erased the memory of it. Or, at least, he thought he did."

"OMG, baby girl, I don't quite know what to say..."

"I was 15, Athena. Dane is not the only one, either. Seems there were several that wanted to pick my fruit without my memory of such.

I'm very much less than happy about this and am very glad to still be a virgin. I guess I do owe that mimic a great big thank you...

There are those that would classify those instances as theft Although I was a willing participant, the erasing of the memory shows intent to steal. Taking it without my knowledge..."

"I have no words..." Tears were streaming down Athena's face. AlaHanDrea hugged her close, then whispered in her ear that she wanted to see Dane, asap.

"Baby girl, we all brought you gifts. These will help you to curve the urges... Tame the hormone beasts... Keep control..." Tootsie told her, then handed her the first one.

All of the other ladies began stacking their gifts next to her. They all laughed when she opened them, trying to figure out what they were for. They explained it to her.

Trena and Dena volunteered to show her how to use them, so the rest of the ladies went outside to join the festivities.

Once the guys understood what was going on inside, they all became very excited, wishing they could go in and help... But, were told to keep out... It was driving them wild!

The girls all loved watching them act like fools...

Chapter 8

"I'd rather not, Athena." Dane told his sister.

"I can understand that, but Dane, you need to go do this. What were you thinking, anyway? She freely gave herself to you, why erase her memory? She was of an acceptable age..."

"Was she really? I guess that's a matter of perspective.

I went to her, truthfully, because I was afraid that Leon was going to take what was mine.

I laid my claim when she was just a baby!

Her fruit was mine to pick.

Fruit, flower, whatever it's being called."

"Oh, Dane.

So, why erase her memory?"

"I didn't want anyone to know. I didn't want her to become all clingy and having expectations of me."

"I thought you loved her..."

"Well, ya, I love her.

She's my baby girl!

That's why I took what was mine to take!

But does that mean I have to spend a bunch of time entertaining her?

I mean, she's real pretty and looks great on my arm.

She's also real powerful and is good to have in emergencies.

We make a good looking couple, for sure.

But, I don't really enjoy drylanders much. Especially on dry land."

"Dane! You sound perfectly horrible!"

"Well, it's the truth!"

"Dane, she was 15? Bro, you had just gotten married!"

"So."

"What do you mean, so? What was all of that big speech about how much you love your wife? And how you want to set a new precedence .. Prove that mers can have long-term, meaningful relationships... I thought you wanted to set an example for others to follow... At least that's what you said..."

"Ya, and? Duh! That's kind of why I didn't want anybody to know."

"When were you planning on telling baby girl that you were married? Y'all already had kids when you went to the island to see her. Why weren't you honest with her then? Dane, you knew before you went to her on that island, that she had gone there, because she was hurting over misuse by men, as well as being upset over stuff she found out from her mother...

Still, you went to her and failed to tell her that you'd gotten married and had children.

How did you think she was going to feel when she found out that she'd spent her time making beautiful love with a married man?

How did you think she'd feel when she discovered you didn't bother to tell her that you'd gotten married and didn't invite her to the wedding, never told her when your children were born...?"

"I don't guess I really gave it much thought. I mean, I figured she'd prolly be all kinds of upset, is why I didn't mention it, really... Would have spoiled the mood for sure!

We had a great time on the islands ... Why ruin a good thing?"

"Little brother, oh, my little brother... How can you be so cold?"

" Dunno... I'm a mer ..."

"Dane, most Mers are not without feelings... DADDY!"

"Uh! Athena! Whatcha calling him for? Ya big tattle tale!"

"Hello Dane, Athena."

"Daddy," they both said in Unison.

Athena did a video playback of the conversation she'd just had with her little brother...

"Seriously Dane? Seriously? You know, you may have been with an imposter, but Baby Girl still knows all of the details.

Looks to me like the jokes on you.

Baby girl remains a virgin and you're in big trouble!

Son, you romanced that girl from the cradle! You sang her songs about growing old with her!

I've stayed away from her, because I didn't want to step on your toes!

You're her Dane! I was shocked when you got married and it wasn't to her."

"Daddy, she's a drylander."

"She's amphibious, son."

"True, but she's still a dry lander with drylander skin! And daddy, we are God's!

"And? I'd gladly take her as a wife! Not a solo wife, but, I'd be honest with her about that right from the start!"

"Really dad? You wanted AlaHanDrea?"

"What do you mean, wanted? Don't you mean, want? Damn straight I want her! What reasonable male doesn't? That girl is the complete package!

And news flash son, she's not the kind of girl you treat the way you've treated that girl!

No girl should be treated like you have treated that girl!

You have no right to recklessly break anyone's heart!

That's straight up cruelty!

Heartless cruelty.

You wouldn't much like it if she did you that way.

Are you forgetting, That girl saved your life???! She was still a toddler and saved your life!

By the laws we all live by, you belong to her, Dane! She plucked you from the jaws of certain death! She owns you!

You owe her!

Huge!"

"I'm not bowing down to her."

"Why not? I will! Are you saying that you're greater than me? Son, I don't quite know how to break this to you, but, you are a demi God. Half Human. Your mother was a human."

"What?"

"You heard me!"

"But Daddy..."

"Yes, son?"

Neptune stood with his arms crossed, tapping his fin on the sand...

"But, but, Daddy..."

"Yes?"

"What I did was wrong.

I really do love her, ya know. I always have.

Truthfully, I've always known that she'd never belong to just me... That's why I got married and made a family. I didn't want to be left standing alone.

I wanted somebody to love me always, like when Baby Girl walks away from me...

My heart has been invested in her, daddy!"

"There's my son. I knew he was in there somewhere.

Tell her what you just told me... No, better yet...

Before you go see her.....,"

"Daddy, what did you just do?"

"I just sent her the video file of the last 40 minutes. You'll stay here with me!"

"Dad, I need to go see my wife."

"Yes, you do. She deserves the truth. She's a good woman. She'll be alright."

———————

"AlaHanDrea, what's wrong?" Tootsie asked her.

King Neptune sent me a video file of a conversation he and Athena had with Dane.

I can't be upset with Dane.

It was not his intention to hurt me.

He's right, too. I doubt I will ever belong to just one male. How can I ever choose?

I love Dane with all my heart... I honestly do.

But I also love Keithen, Braynar, Danalli, Kenneth, Franklon, etc... Etc... Etc ...

When I'm alone with them, I'm sure they are the one I want, until I see one of the others ...

Danes right. He's vulnerable and just trying to protect himself."

"What are you going to do?"

"Go see Dane," AlaHanDrea said, then stopped herself... "Just not now..."

The teen queen held her head up high, walked outside, then said, " alright, who will drum for me? I believe I'd like to dance, or sing or something."

The music started, AlaHanDrea began to sing. Her voice was so beautiful. " Life is so good when there is love... Life is best when there is love..."

A male voice joined in, a very familiar, male voice...

"When a boy loves a girl, then the man loves the woman ... the way this man loves the woman in love with her man.. and her man is me.... Yes , her man is me....oh can't you see... Her man is me....."

They both fell silent. Dane walked over to her, pulled her into his arms and began dancing with her.

They finished the song without saying a word. As the song ended, Dane kissed her with pure, honest love ... At the end of the kiss, Dane looked deeply into her eyes, then said, "I love you from the depth of my soul and with all of my heart! I love you like I love none other. No other love compares to the love I have for you, my baby queen...

Youth and fear caused mistakes, mistakes that caused un necessary pain, and for that, I am truly apologetic. Please, forgive me. It's not my intention to ever hurt you.

I've come to realize that we must love each other enough to allow each other to live our lives.

I didn't take a wife because I don't love you... because I do love you

...

I took a wife so I could deal with living without you.

I love my wife. Just not the same way that I Love you. There is just no comparison.

My wife knows how I feel and she's good with it. She's a mermaid."

AlaHanDrea hugged Dane and held him close.

They stood there, holding each other while the music played on. There wasn't a dry eye in the crowd.

Dane let go, looked her in the eye, smiled, then spun her around and began dancing with her. The drummers stepped up the beat...

Keithen, Danalli, Braynar and Thomlin began singing the prettiest songs! Tootsie jumped up and in the Style of AlaHanDrea, Sang a beautiful verse that cracked everyone up, especially Dane and AlaHanDrea!

Dane went up and joined the men, while AlaHanDrea, Isabel and Cathey Ann went up to join Tootsie.

Midway through the song, the ladies switched and sang a verse that brought a tear to the eye, so the guys took over on the laughs.

The audience was rolling in laughter!

The rest of the night was spent laughing with friends, dancing and making beautiful music, until the darkness was gone and sunlight began to signal the beginning of a new day...

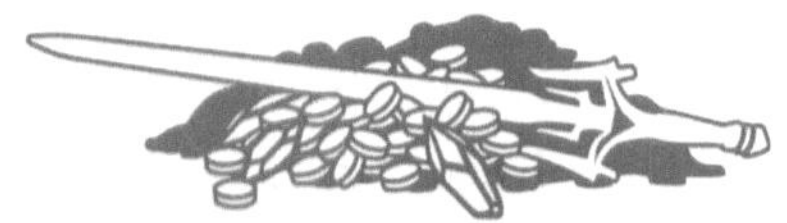

Chapter 9

"AlaHanDrea, you wanted to see me?" Tootsie asked the teen queen.

"Yes. I have something weighing heavily on my mind. I'm hoping that you can help me figure it all out..."

"Well, I can certainly try. What's up?"

"There are far too many human and humanoid orphan's.

Humans are supposed to be so sophisticated and civilized, yet, they don't even care for their own children.

It's come to my attention that humans even kill unborn children after mating successfully.

I mean, I can understand that circumstances exist that make the practice necessary in certain situations, however, inconvenience should not not be on that list.."

"I know, it's really sad. How can I help?"

"I want to open a ranch for orphans, as well as pregnant girls that don't want their babies, so they don't have to kill the unborn for lack of being able care for them."

"How do you plan to pull this off?"

"Well, that's where you come in. I'd like for you to sell some of my treasures and purchase land, preferably a couple or three islands close to shore.

We want a place for orphans coming of age to move to, in the mix.

We need schools, hospitals, shopping... We need to build 'Orphan Islands'... Complete villages.

We want to offer families a home to live in, as an exchange for taking care of the children. The houses will come with the orphans....

We need tons of farm and ranch space as well, so probably some mainland farms and ranches."

"AlaHanDrea, this is a huge undertaking, how much treasure have you got?"

"As much as you need, and more. I'm sure I can count on dragon kind for regular donation of more treasure...

I need you to be the boss of it all. Recruit who you need, as long as they have prince or princess in their name, for the lead positions.

I think it should always be operated by princes and princesses."

"So, I run the show? The whole show?"

"Yes. It's your baby.

Do you think it will be difficult to gather a team together that can get this project underway?" The teen queen asked.

"No, not really, I think it's a great project! I actually think that once you get the ball rolling, the humans will jump on board with it.

So, are you going to handle the initial announcements and advertising, or, is that my department as well?"

"I don't mind making announcements, but that's about as involved as it gets.

Isabel gave me some rather disturbing news that I need to deal with."

"Is it anything you wish to talk about?"

"Tootsie, Isabel has my parents locked up in Chambers, waiting for me and has had them in there for a bit."

"Well, now, I heard that your mom got a new body to live in, but you said parents?"

"Yes. Mom And Dad! I've never known anything about my father. I'm not sure that I want to."

"Well, of course, you want to! You pretty much have to! Want me to go with you?"

"Yes, please."

"You got it, sweetheart! When would you like to go?"

"Well, I was kinda thinking about right now."

"Oh! O.k. well, would you also like for Cathey Ann to go as well?"

"Sure, why not. I'll summon her."

"Ya don't have to, she's right outside. She was with me when I came, she got sidetracked by a royal pain, I mean, Prince Keithen."

"You had it right the first time!" AlaHanDrea told her, making them both giggle.

Isabel, Tootsie and Cathey Ann seemed about as nervous as AlaHanDrea did, as they went to the chamber holding the teen Queens parents, stopping right outside the door for a moment.

"AlaHanDrea, both of your parents are here, however, your mom and dad have not seen each other yet, per your mother's request. You may have to push that to happen. Are you ready to go in and meet your father?"

"No, not really, but, I suppose I have to do this..."

The royal guard's opened the double doors to the chamber. AlaHanDrea took a deep breath, readying herself to go in when she heard a voice telling her to wait. It was Leon and Danalli. Braynar wasn't far behind.

They caught up with her and took her hands in theirs...

"AlaHanDrea, no matter what happens, know that you are loved, wanted and that you are absolutely perfect the way you are.

Should anger try to join you, remind yourself that these are the ones that made you!"

"I love you guys! Let's go in there!"

Isabel went in first. "AlaHanDrea, I'd like for you to meet Jeffry, your father."

The two just stood there, staring at one another, not speaking, just staring. Finally, after about ten minutes, Tootsie grabbed AlaHanDrea's upper arm, about to speak to her, when she heard them speaking ... They were speaking without saying a word with their mouths! As long as Tootsie had a ahold of baby girls arm, she could hear them!

Tootsie put Leon's hand on Alahandrea's arm for him to hear, the others followed suit.

AlaHanDrea didn't seem to notice, she was preoccupied.

Cathey Ann slipped out and went into Folica's chamber. What ever she said to Folica worked, because moments later, Folica walked into the chamber, then froze in her tracks.

"Who is she?" Jeffry asked.

"I'm Folica."

"No you're not! You look nothing at all like Folica! No where near the right species blends... Do I look stupid or something?"

"I am Folica. I was given a new body to live in since I killed the first body I had. Now, I'm a kitty cat."

"Folica? Seriously? My sweet, beautiful Folica?

Girl, we were both so young! I didn't mean to be such a jerk when you told me you were pregnant! I was scared! I've been miserable without you! There hasn't been a single day that I haven't regretted my actions....

I should never have given up pestering you!

You just don't look like my Folica!"

"Jeffry, I was in the lab, heard someone coming and hid myself. You walked in and greeted me, said I was doing a lousy job at hiding.

You kissed me and were going to show me sex, but the scientists were coming!

Jeffry, when you showed it to me, I giggled!"

"It is you!

Oh Folica!"

Jeffry ran to her and took her in his arms, hugging her like he never wanted to let her go.

AlaHanDrea started to turn and leave the room, when her father reached out and took her arm. His arm stretched like the rapidly growing branch of a tree, all of the way across the room and took ahold of her arm!

"Not so fast, there, young lady."

He pulled her over to them.

Her group of chaperones stood in awe...

They had never seen a creature like her father & had no idea what to think of him!

They all quietly turned and stepped outside, closed the doors and took a seat. They wanted to give the newly united family space, but had absolutely no intention of going anywhere.

They all wanted to be close by in case AlaHanDrea needed them.

They were all startled by the sound of somebody hurriedly coming up the path, quickly approaching them... It was JayDe.

"Braynar, there you are! I was looking for you."

"Hi there little buddy, you look frazzled "

"Yeah well, I kind of got into a bit of a scrape with some humans. They were chasing me. Okay so, I did kill a fella, but dang it, I'm a werewolf, it's what we do!"

Everyone chuckled. "We're not laughing at you, little buddy, we're laughing with you. Everyone here completely understands what you're going through! It's in our nature to kill humans!

We have had to come up with compromises in order to live together in peace.

We try to stick to the humans that stink of sin.

Some of us keep humans for pets.

In more recent years, we have developed ranches for humans, to make it easier to fill our food supply.

We've taken humans given to us as food and use them for breeding purposes, to develop our ranches from humans that would not exist had we eaten their parents.

It works for us.

We got the idea from the humans.

They have huge ranches full of livestock.

Now, we do too.

It seems to me that we need to come up with a way for you to fulfill your bloodlust and not get chased down by angry humans." Braynar explained.

"Can I have a job at one of your ranches?" JayDe asked while laughing.

Everyone else had to laugh with him on that one.

"Ya know guys, I really love my life here on Taurus 9! Y'all rock! I used to be so depressed over what I am, y'all have taught me to embrace what I am and be proud of me, thank you all!"

"Ah, we're all glad to have you here among us!" Isabel told him, then kissed his cheek, making him blush.

The double doors opened, Jeffry was distraught... "AlaHanDrea vanished." He cried.

"Oh no! What did you say to her to make her want to run away?" Isabel asked.

"I don't know! I honestly don't know! She said, Leon! While looking at Folica and vanished!"

Leon got a sinking feeling in his gut....

Everyone there knew what that meant...

"Folica must have been thinking about Leon and she picked it up!" Danalli commented.

"Oh no, this is bad, really bad..." Isabel said, then, "guards, keep Baby Girls parents in chamber and don't let them out! I'll be back!"

"Yes, your majesty."

"WELL, ANY LUCK?" ISABEL asked as the group come back in.

"Not really, but then, we saw a storm brewing and if I were to guess, I would think she's directly under it," Braynar said.

"Truthfully, I think she's causing it!" Danalli commented.

"I need to go see her and talk to her, but I'm probably the last one she wants to see right now. But, that's really just too bad for her. She's going to listen to me!" Leon announced, then headed for the storm....

"JAYDE CAN I SEE YOU for a moment? The rest of y'all, too," Tootsie asked.

"Sure, what's up?"

Tootsie explained the orphans islands idea to the whole group,

"JayDe, you are the only one of your kind on this planet, correct?"

"Ya, why?"

Isabel saw where she was going with it...

"JayDe, under Dragon Law and the law set forth by the watchers, you are hereby known as King JayDe," Isabel declared.

Braynar produced a nice crown... placing it on JayDe took some modifying....

"How about that! I'm royalty! If that don't beat all! I was an outcast on Beta Centauri. On Taurus 9, I'm a king!

Tootsie spoke up, "yes, you are and as such, I'm hoping you can see your way clear to govern over security for the orphans project."

"Wow! Really? You want me to be in charge of security?!

"I actually think you're perfect for it!"

"I'm honored! Wow! Look at me! I'm a King AND I'm in charge of something important! Will wonders never cease!"

Chapter 10

"Go away, Leon, just go away!" AlaHanDrea barked at the distraught Prince.

" I will not go away and you are going to listen to me!

For one thing, I was under a spell, AlaHanDrea!

You don't know the whole truth!

Before you go judging and jumping to conclusions, you need to hear the facts!

Now, look here, I love you to pieces and I know what this looks like, but woman!"

Leon pushed against the wall of strong wind the upset teen queen threw at him.

When he reached her, he grabbed her by the upper arms and pulled her close, wrapped his arms around her, successfully pinning her.

"Now, you listen to me, you hear me and you hear me good!

I was drugged!

And!

A spell was Cast on me!

I would have NEVER done the things I did, had I been in my right mind!

YOU CAN BE MAD AT ME ALL YOU WANT TO! But you're only this upset because you love me! And, I love you!

So, you're just going to have to be mad while you're lovin me... Today, I'm giving you a gift that will last... a gift that lets me be part of you always ... so, stop your squirming, because I'm not letting you go!

And I'm not taking no for an answer either!

You're getting this and that's all there is to it!

Truthfully, I should have already done this a big long time ago!

Now, Stop fighting me!" he scolded, then kissed her with love and passion.

At the end of the kiss, he placed restraints on her wrists!"

"Is all of this really necessary?" She asked him with a sarcastic tone.

"Absolutely.

It makes it easier for me to do what I need to do! Now, AlaHanDrea, I said, stop struggling!

We've talked about this and I know you want it!

Now, I'm doing this and that's all there is to it!" he looked deep into her eyes, then kissed her eyes, then her lips, so softly.

His kisses trailed down her neck and shoulder, then back up to her lips, as he lit fires deep inside of her.

Leon could feel her reacting.

Passion and desire were building inside of her!

He was trying to be careful not to light anything he couldn't put out.

Leon was very skilled & careful, taking his time with her.

He wanted to make sure it was a special and memorable event for her.

"Woman, I have been in love with you since you were just a few days old.

I love you, and, woman! Today, you belong to me! I'm taking what's mine! and what's more, you're going to love it!" He kissed her again....

The storm turned to a gentle rain with a double rainbow.

———————

"Hey mom, look, Leon found her and from the looks of things, he's got her in a much better mood.

How much ya wanna bet she's no longer a ....."

"Braynar! Watch that mouth! But, since you brought it up, I'll bet you're wrong!

So, how much ya willing to bet?" Isabel asked her oldest son.

"Your majesty, I'd be glad to fly over and break that party up, just say the word!" Danalli volunteered.

"That won't be necessary. Let them work this out..." Isabel told him.

"LEON, I DO LOVE YOU!

I really do love you!

Are we really going to do this?"

"Yes, ma'am, we are.

Just relax and trust me.

Now, it's going to hurt a little, probably going to sting, so hold real still, it won't take me too terribly long... now, don't move!" he instructed. "Trust me baby, I'm an expert, I'll do it right, don't you worry yourself even one little bit.

The first time is always the hardest. The anxiety of it is the hardest part.

It's natural to be a little scared.

Here, drink this potion. It will help with the anxiety, as well as the pain. Go ahead, drink it all up now, that's right."

"I'm Not Scared! That stuff tastes funny," she giggled. "Hey, I feel real weeeee!

OUCH! Hey! That hurts!

You're right!

It does hurt and it Does sting, ouch!"

"Oh, stop your whining! I'll be through in a few minutes or so! Hold still, now! Would you like some more potion?"

"Leon, that is really painful! Yes, a bigger serving please! Liquid courage is a good thing!"

"Yes,, it can get you through some tough stuff... are you going to talk through this whole thing? I need to focus on what I'm doing ...

Now, now, the worst is almost over, you're doing fine... that's right, just relax and hold still, baby, I'm making it hurt as little as possible, I promise!

Take some deep breaths, long slow deep breaths... just a bit longer.... you're really doing fine! Oh sweetheart, you're doing just great!

Now, the worst is done...this last part doesn't sting nearly as much, but it takes a bit longer... now be still!

Ya, right like that!

Wow, you're doing great! A real trooper!

I knew you'd do great!

"Me talking? That's you putting out all the words! I'm holding still, Leon, but damnit! I had no idea it would hurt this much!"

"Do you want me to stop?"

"No, your not through! You have to finish!"

"It won't hurt much longer. It may be sore for a couple or a few days, but you'll be alright and wanting to do it again!

Almost done, now, stop your squirming.

Almost finished!

Almost there!

Ok, hold real still, as still as you possibly can for this part!

Are you ready?

Almost there!

That's it!

Yes!

Yes, baby!

Just like that!

Whew...

There, now, all done...

See, that wasn't so bad, now was it?

Let me get you all cleaned up..there's just a little bit of blood, but that's natural...."

"No, it wasn't really that bad, I just wasn't expecting it to be so painful. "

"Ya, the first time is always the worst, next time you'll know what to expect.

Now, others are going to want to do this, too.

Promise you'll come to me first, so I can make sure it's done right. Come on now, promise me!"

"Thank you Leon! Thank you so much! And yes, I promise to come to you first.

Oh my sweet baby, You're forever a part of me now!"

"Yes, I am. There's no taking that back! It's pretty permanent..."

"Can I look now?"

"Sure, go ahead."

"Oh!

Leon!

It's absolutely beautiful!

Oh, it's just gorgeous!

Oh Leon!

Thank you, thank you thank you, baby!

I Love my flying lion!

You are always with me now!

Oh Leon!

You made my upper arm so pretty!

Red, but very pretty! You are really a great artist!

But dang baby, tattoos hurt!"

"Yes, that, they do!"

"Thank you for using subtle colors..."

"You're welcome baby girl... Let's go show off your new art!"
"Sure, but first, I need some details about all of that mess...."
"Of course. Of course you do!"

Chapter 11

Isabel had been pacing the floor for the best part of fifteen minutes when Braynar and Jason walked in.

"Jason, please go fetch King JayDe Blackwolf for me."

*At once, your majesty," Jason replied.

"Braynar, it's high time you and Danalli begin to take over some of the duties of the king....

Begin the slow process of transitioning..." Isabel told her oldest son.

"Seriously, mother?" Braynar asked, surprised.

"Don't you think you're ready?"

"Yes ma'am, Im sure that we both are," Braynar replied.

"I've decided, excuse me, you and Danalli have decided, that JayDe's department become part of the Royal Guard with King JayDe Blackwolf as the top Dog... pun intended... " She giggled.

"Well, now, when you put it that way, I suppose he is top dog! Yes ma'am, so, that would be why you sent for him, rather than simply summon him?"

"Correct. Tootsie is on her way as well."

"Danalli?" Braynar asked.

"I sure hope so!" Isabel responded.

"Oh great! It looks like everyone is arriving right on time. Y'all come on over and take seats..." Braynar Instructed the newly formed crowd.

"JayDe, if you'd be so kind as to step over here for a just a moment please?

Ya, stand right over here, ya, that's fine, right there.." Isabel instructed.

"As the future kings of all of Drakonia as well as Taurus 9, Prince Braynar and Prince Danalli, on this day, have a decree.... "

"King JayDe Blackwolf, IT IS HEREBY DECREED that your department of Security be of and hereby is, a division of, The Royal Guard! With you at the helm for leadership, guidance, and inspiration.

You answer directly to the throne.

You, are Top Dog over your branch of security/guards   From this day forward, so says I, Prince Braynar, heir to the throne."...

"So says I Prince Danalli, Heir to the throne."

"So says I, Queen Isabel St George, Reigning Queen."

"Congratulations were given by all present.

"Wow! I'm part of the royal guard! wow!" JayDe said, astonished at the honor.

"I really love it here!" JayDe was honestly happy for the first time in his entire life!

"AlaHanDrea's party is on the schedule. So, who is going to be the one to be her date for the evening?"

Isabel asked.

"I'm not sure she'd agree to go on the arm of a werewolf..." JayDe commented.

"Well, I think it should be me," Braynar said.

"Why you and not me?" Danalli asked.

"Why either of you when I'm here," Kenneth said as he entered their area.

Craigen couldn't help himself, "age before beauty, fellas!"

"Excuse me, if I might butt in for a moment..." Leon said as he walked up...

"I do believe it's kitty night... Have y'all noticed baby girls tattoo?" He boasted.

"Wait, you gave her a tattoo?" Braynar exclaimed.

"Sure did!" Leon bragged...

AlaHanDrea walked up to the group ...

"Hi fellas! Hello Isabel!" She seemed cheerful.

"AlaHanDrea, have you chosen a date for your party yet?" Isabel asked.

"Why should I be made to choose? Look at all of these fine specimens... How could any lady possibly choose between these men? Maybe a contest should decide."

"I have a great idea!" JayDe said. "Let the viewers decide! Broadcast this. Give each man time to talk about himself and why he is the best choice as escort. Then, let the audience vote!"

"Oh, that's a great idea, JayDe!" Isabel said. "This must happen today. Make it so."

"Yes your majesty."

"Well, C'Mon guys, let's get this show on the road!" JayDe told the group.

Huge viewing screens popped up all over.

"Greetings and pardon the intrusion into your day.

Queen AlaHanDrea here. A party is being thrown in my honor, to welcome me home from captivity.

A problem has arisen that I need your help with...

I cannot choose a date. They are all much too magnificent to have to choose one myself, so, I'm asking all y'all to please choose for me!

The possible suitors will take turns introducing themselves, then y'all can vote on who I should go with!

Thank you in advance for your help with this!

I'm so excited!"

Braynar went first, then Danalli. Danalli pulled out all the stops and showed videos of the two of them in battle together...

In almost no time at all, a long line of males stood waiting for a turn to explain why they would be a good choice!

"Isabel! Look at All the handsome men!" The teen queen exclaimed.

Females began to gather in groups, staring at the guys, giggling and talking about them.... Openly Flirting ... Many of them were enticed to go with some of the young ladies that showed up. They probably decided the competition was too strong and went for the sure thing. Of course the young ladies were all very pretty.... None of them were a second choice type girl...

All of a sudden, the sound of blaring horns filled the air, signaling an emergency evacuation of the planets surface!

Danalli shifted just in time for AlaHanDrea to climb on his neck. Braynar was already in the air, as were the royal guard's, Keithen, Kenneth, George and Thomlin. Craigen was getting there as fast as he could fly.

Creatures scattered into the catacombs below the planets surface... Hunkering down to await word....

More aliens! They seemed to possess a level of manners, taking orbit just outside of the upper atmosphere. Their numbers were unbelievably large!

As soon as the dragons saw how many of them were there, they called for all creatures to take cover! No one was to be above the surface... No one!

AlaHanDrea put up communication screens and demanded they leave at once!

"Hi, I'm Admiral Charlie Mathis, from Sagittarius 11 in the outer Keiper belt of the Milky Way Galaxy, approximately 4 star systems away from yours.

We wish to colonize your planet."

"Ya, that's not going to be happening!" AlaHanDrea told the alien Admiral.

"We are not asking your permission, we are simply notifying you of what Is Happening. As you can tell, we are a quite advanced people! We no longer have the need of riding on the backs of beasts," the admiral's sarcasm was obvious.

"Another stupid alien that thinks their superior because you learned how fly around in space.

Well, bully for you!

You can space travel!

Oh boy!

I hate to be the one to tell you this, but you are so not advanced...

Maybe compared to cave men, you are, but look at you, still using ships to crawl around in space....

And so slowly, too!

We ride on beasts because we enjoy it, Admiral Smart Ass!

Admiral dumb ass is more like it!

Attention crew of Admiral Dumb Ass, if you care to evacuate the ship prior to it's destruction, we will gladly accommodate you and assist you to go back where you've come from. It won't take very long, you can be back by breakfast in the morning... Or, stay here, with this rude idiot and die.

The choice is yours, but, make no mistake, this ship is most certainly doomed," AlaHanDrea explained.

The lead alien ship began vibrating and heating up!

The admiral was like a statue, only his eye could move! They had lost control of their ship! None of their controls worked! Terror filled the ships!

Hundreds of aliens began begging for mercy as their mother ship began shaking apart!

Approximately 10,000 aliens, total, between the ships, all begging to go home....

Only a handful begged for mercy as well as asylum.

The crew was searched for shape shifters. Over 375 were located and transported to the surface.

The remainder of the population were being transported home by the watchers. All except a few hundred, begging to stay on Taurus 9.

George went in to address the 375 shape shifters... "Y'all were chosen out of the entire populace ... Y'all were chosen and will remain on Taurus 9.

Welcome home, brethren!" King George announced, then shifted into dragon state.

Terrified aliens screamed in horror when they saw George shift.

He quickly shifted back, then walked over to them to have a closer look at them.

"y'all don't know who and what you are! You honestly don't know, do you?"

The aliens were all huddled together, trembling in fear.

"Brethren, fear not, you are home now.

Safe.

Right where you belong...

Do you not know that you are dragons?

Do you not suffer from strange dreams?

Wow, y'all have been suppressed for so long, you no longer know who and what you are!

Don't be frightened! We are kin.

Please tell me, why did your admiral come here to colonize this planet?" George asked them.

"Freedom." They all answered at once.

"We came to the new world in search of freedom." One of the ladies spoke up.

"Your admiral seems to be unaware of his bad manners. It's not right to barge into someone else's world as though it's ok to just move right in, simply because you desire to do so.

Did your leader discuss what to do about the current inhabitants?
" George asked.

"Yes, he said that if y'all objected, he'd simply kill you all!" One of
the ladies spoke up.

"What arrogance! Such disregard for life!" George commented.

"You can do what ever you want to do to us, but you have to
understand some thing, the people of our planet know where we have
come to and they will retaliate our deaths!" one of the men said.

Another spoke up, " What do you mean, we are Kin?"

"I mean just that. We have the same ancestors. You are just like us...
or, used to be... it looks to me like they tried to breed it out of you."

"Your majesty, I'm sorry to disturb you, but a group of the alien
humans don't want to return to their planet. They say they'd rather be
executed than to return. I explained to them that we don't wish to end
their lives without good reasons to do so, but they don't want to go
back!" Kenneth told the king.

"Take them to quarantine."

"Yes, your majesty, as you wish."

"So, king, you're like the ruler over your kingdom?"

"I'm like ruler over this planet."

"So, the ruler over this entire planet speaks to us?"

"Is there some reason why I shouldn't?"

"How do you know we won't kill you?"

George cracked up laughing. "Oh, you're funny! You are really Mr.
Funny man!

So Much to learn!

You don't even remember how to shift or use your magic and you
think you have the power to kill the mightiest dragon on the planet!
Oh, you're too funny! You're also lucky we don't execute stupidity.

Guards! Do something with these idiots, please. Feel free to eat a
few of them, should you choose to. I'd recommend starting with mr
mouth over there."

"Yes, your majesty. Uh, your majesty, do we have anymore dipping sauce? These ones look to be a bit sour..." Craigen asked, jokingly.

It was all George could do to keep a straight face. "Ya, uh, I think the girls left some behind that wall, if they didn't use it all up when they ate the last load of smart assed aliens... what ever you do, don't take too long. The party starts soon.

I sure hope you're well rested, Craigen!

The mermaids are coming and you know what that means!"

"I'll, be there with bells on!"

"She still making you wear bells? Damn man!" George teased.

"Na, we are not together anymore."

"What happened, I kinda liked that one..." George continued to play along.

"She opened her mouth, stupid fell out... Ate her!"

"Ah, o.k. well, good then. See ya at the party!"

George cracked up the second he stepped out of earshot. He loved his men and their sense of humors....

George ran into Raynar once he was outside.

"Raynar, did Jax Transport the others?" George asked.

"He's the supervising watcher. Dad sent troops."

"Ah! That's why conquering these aliens was so easy."

"Yes. They were surrounded in a way they couldn't defend against.

I suppose that's one of the perks to having so much watcher royalty on the planets surface."

"Nice perk!"

"So George, have you had time to visit with AlaHanDrea since she's been back?"

"No, I, uh , I, uh..."

"Embarrassed?"

"Ya."

"You do realize that the mimic used magic on you, don't you?"

"It did?"

"Yes, it did. It caused you to act on your secret desires. It wanted to experience everything, as well as get a good grip on the king of the world."

"Well, ya, that makes sense."

"Feel better?"

"Yes, I do, thank you for telling me that."

"You're welcome. Now, go see AlaHanDrea."

"I suppose I should. Do you know where she is?"

George vanished!

Raynar shook his head with a grin on his face, knowing that AlaHanDrea had just summoned George...

"Hello sweet girl, I was just talking to Ray about you," George said to AlaHandrea.

"George, I think we need to talk."

"Wow! you look absolutely stunning!"

"Thank you, George. I know what happened with the mimic and I already know about it using magic on you. But, I also know that it only brought your desires to the surface. Your unspoken desires to the surface."

George was blushing deep red and swallowed hard. AlaHanDrea walked over and stood in front of him, looking into his eyes. Neither of them so much as blinked. Before he knew what he was doing, he was kissing her and she was kissing him back.

He looked deeply into her eyes again, searching ... Then kissed her again, with much more passion.

"George, you are an exquisite man! You take my breath away! I need you to know something, George, I do love you, I always have!

As a girl, I dreamed of being together with you.

You are not the only one with unspoken desires!

You're not alone in your feelings. I just need for you to know that!

Right now, I'm still a virgin, but I won't always be.

Our day will come, George, our day will come! Our lives are long on this world and our day WILL come."

George had a big smile on his face. Thank you, Baby Girl. I needed to hear this. I really needed to hear this! You're amazing, you know that?" He asked, then kissed her again, followed by a long hug.

"AlaHanDrea, I love you deep in my heart! Precious girl, you're a part of me forever, already.

I can't imagine my life without you in it, nor do I want to try!

My life was made better the day you arrived on this planet. Please know that I'm always here for you! Always."

"Thank you, my love. One more kiss?"

"Of course...!"

Chapter 12

"Queen Isabel, the votes have been counted! You're not going to believe the outcome! You're just not going to believe it!" Kenneth said.

"Why, who won?"

"Your majesty, he didn't even speak! Yet, he was voted in!"

"Who?"

"Tommy!"

"What?"

"It's a landslide victory! Tommy!"

"Ah, you've got to be kidding?!"

"Nope, not in the least. It's unanimous, by a huge margin! Tommy won!"

Tommy had beads of sweat on his forehead and was gripping the bouquet of flowers he was carrying, rather tightly, as he nervously walked up the path to AlaHanDrea's home. He still couldn't believe that he was chosen to be her escort!

AlaHanDrea had no clue who had been chosen. It remained a surprise for her. Cameras were hovering above Tommy in order to catch the moment for all to see.

A single door stood in a free standing frame at the edge of her home area.

Tommy chuckled when he saw it just standing there, as if it somehow belonged...

He knew it was there to hide his identity until the very last moment, so, he stood up close to it and knocked.

Excitement filled AlaHanDrea when she heard the knocking...

Still, she walked slowly over to the door, wearing a gorgeous white flowing cloak with a white fur trimmed, billowing hood.

The cloaks train drug the ground, so tiny fairies gathered around it's edge to carry it and keep it up out of the dirt.

AlaHanDrea was so nervous to see who was chosen for her... (She hadn't seen Tommy since she had returned).

The door slowly opened. Not a sound was heard across the planet as all eyes were on that door, slowly opening to reveal AlaHanDrea's escort to her.

Once the door opened, the look of shock on her face was priceless! She didn't recognize him at first. Tommy handed her the flowers... The tiny fairies took them and put them in a vase of water for her.

"AlaHanDrea, it's me, Tommy. I grew up!"

"Tommy? Tommy! Wow! Look at you! OMG! Tommy! Wow! Look at you! Oh Tommy! It's so good to see you! You won! Wow! It's been a few years, but, Wow! I didn't recognize you at first!"

"Ya, I've changed a bunch, and... I didn't even compete! I didn't think I was allowed to compete, but wow, AlaHanDrea, look at how gorgeous you are! We're all grown up!"

"Yes, we sure are! May I please have a hug?"

"I can do ya one better than that!" He said as he took her in his arms and kissed her so sweetly.

Cheers could be heard like thunder from all across the land.

The cheering turned to chanting... TOMMY, TOMMY, TOMMY! Followed by more cheers.

The two of them stood gazing into each other's eyes, smiling at one another.

"Shall we?" Tommy asked, offering her his arm...

"Wow! Tommy, I mean, wow!" She was amazed at the man he'd grown into... "So, you didn't compete?"

."No, for some reason, I didn't think I was supposed to compete... But then, I heard on the broadcast that I was a write in vote!

I'm so glad that I was!" Tommy stopped and turned to look at AlaHandrea eye to eye...

"Since we were kids, AlaHanDrea, since we were just kids..." He said, then kissed her again. He straightened himself up, stood back next to her, and prepared to be presented...

"PRESENTING PRINCE TOMMY! AND HIS ESCORT, THE ONE, THE ONLY, TEEN QUEEN, QUEEN ALA HAN DREA!!!

The applause rose like thunder. As Queen AlaHanDrea stepped forward, her cloak remained in the hands of tiny fairies, hanging in the air as if she were still inside ... The thunderous applause became deafening at the site of AlaHanDrea in the sequin spiral gown with rows of sheer between the sequins, fitting snuggly against her curves and crevices, then flowing to the floor, but slit up the left side to her hip. Spaghetti straps held the elongated triangle breast pieces, attached to the skirt at the waist... Criss crossing across her back ... The gown sparkled of jewels, top to bottom.

Her flaming red and gold curly hair was half up, woven around her crown... Her gloves stopped at the elbow so as to not cover her tattoo...

Her crystal high heals sparkled of diamond anklets...

She was an absolute Beauty! The fairies had seen to it!

Tommy was speechless, lost in her beauty, as she waved to the crowd.... He was thankful he'd already kissed her, before he saw her uncloaked!

Tommy fell to his knee and the crowd went silent .

Tommy took AlaHanDrea's hand in his, with the formality due a queen, and kissed her knuckles, pledging his loyalty to her.

There wasn't a dry eye in the house when she helped him to stand back up, then she curtsied to him.... The music began and Tommy pulled her into a dancing stance, then began dancing her across the floor. Much to AlaHanDrea's surprise, her childhood friend had become quite the refined dancer...

The teen queen couldn't help but to notice how well Tommy's tuxedo fit him...

The young couple danced about 4 1/2 songs before deciding to take a seat for a rest.

AlaHanDrea took a drink of nectar, then jumped up and slapped the mug from Tommy's hands before passing out. Tommy caught her as she fell towards the ground.

Security rushed forward, putting Tommy in protective custody, seized all of the nectar barrels as well as the serving dishes and all creatures that were in contact with the nectars and dishes.

Healix arrived instantly ... She was alive, but her breathing was shallow. He had to determine what kind of poison and why...

The cameras were still hovering, they seemed to have multiplied...

Healix jumped backwards when he saw AlaHanDrea rise up out of her own body, but still flash n blood! She stood beside herself for a moment, then placed her hand on the forehead of her body, laying down on the hammock. She looked at Healix for a moment, then began acting like it was normal for her to be doing that!

"Healix, we need to find out why my own parents poisoned me. Not to worry, I won't allow any part of me to die.

But, we need to find my parents and find out why they want me dead."

"AlaHanDrea, how'd you do that?"

"Oh that? That's easy... Look here, I have no intention of missing my own party!"

The roar of the crowd was once again deafening! AlaHanDrea turned and waved to the spectators.....

Security was greatly increased while JayDe himself went in search of the teen Queens parents...

AlaHanDrea won a lot of hearts when she made the party continue....

The triplets all showed up, with their husbands. They loved showing off their skills! That party was a great opportunity for them to be seen worldwide and they took it!

Of course, no one minded, they were incredible entertainment!

The triplets inspired acrobatic figure skating on wheels, planet wide!

"Anything they can do, we can do better!" Could be heard being sung, as a group of dragons showed up, in human state, wheels on their feet and ready to go!

A second dance floor appeared with the bandstand between them....

The show really took off when the music once again, began...

Tommy and AlaHanDrea would join in the fun from time to time, doing Aerial stunts with wheels on their feet... Then taking a seat, visiting with other creatures, mostly royalty... All on camera ......

The human population were continually amazed at how sophisticated and refined the beast population was!

They seemed far more civilized than the humans, themselves, seemed to be....

The beasts seemed far more social, as well as musical... not to mention, spiritual, than the human population... they had an unshakable belief and faith in God ...

Their communities seemed to be far more connected...

Their sense of community was inspiring....

Crime was a non-issue.

The laws of nature prevailed.

A world of predator and prey is not easy in social standards...

So, the beasts adapted.

They developed ranches to fix the food supply... It eased the tensions between certain species....

Where there's a will, there is a way also....

The broadcast of the celebration proved to be very enlightening for everyone.... Future broadcasted happening were a given!

The world couldn't get enough of watching the lives of the beasts....

AlaHanDrea and Tommy were having so much fun! The time flew by and all too soon, it was time to end the date, as night stepped aside for the new day.

The predawn hours were some of AlaHanDrea's favorite moments of the day.

Neither of them were ready for the date to end.

Tommy walked his date home, then waited patiently while she changed into her day clothes. He used his magic to change his own attire.

The fairies showed up with breakfast suitable for Tommy to enjoy.

A group of wolves showed up to see if Tommy wanted to take AlaHanDrea on a run...

Prince Kai, aka The General, put AlaHanDrea on his shoulder, while Tommy rode on another...

The run was exhilarating!

Tommy finally suggested they go down under, go checkout King Neptune's resort. The royal guard was having a bit of a time keeping up with the kids, but the cameras didn't miss a beat!

A feast was served below in the tunnels, then another feast was served after dark up on the island.

Rhythm drums and musicians filled the evening air with beautiful melodies...

A second night of dancing, only much more intimate than the dancing of the night before.

"Oh Tommy, I've had such a great time! What a wonderful way to see you again!"

"Yeah... It's a dream come true for me... AlaHanDrea, I have always loved you so... When the cave in happened back on Ion 6, I was afraid I'd never see you again... We seemed to grow apart ... But, I had no idea she was an imposter! I feel like I should have known!"

"Why should you have known? Mimics are dangerous, because you can't tell!"

"Imagine how close we'd already be, had we been allowed to be in love with each other from way back..."

"Tommy, I do love you! I love you different from any other! But please, understand, I'm not human. I never want to hurt you. Please know, I will not ever belong to only one man. I could not ever possibly choose! Please don't ever ask me to. I need you in my life, always."

Tommy sat for a moment, as though he'd been slapped, but then, he thought about it and smiled. "So, I'm one of your favorite guys?"

"Damned Straight you are!"

"I'm good with that!"

He said, then pulled her to him and kissed her with love and passion. She wrapped her arms around him and kissed him back.

They became lost in one another, seeming to forget about the cameras for a bit.

But when Tommy began to get a little carried away, AlaHanDrea stopped him.

"Tommy, we are not yet ready to become parents, we cannot make a baby right now. As much as I'd love to, and I would love to, neither one of us are ready to become parents."

"Well, I can't argue with that logic."

"Trust me when I tell you, I don't want to stop!"

Tommy kissed her again, then leaned up and looked in her eyes, "are you sure you're not ready for a baby Tommy?"

Then went right back to kissing her.

She got up and stood up. "Now Tommy..." He stood up and pulled her back close ... and she vanished!

"I guess no meant no!" Tommy said out loud, to the viewers...

With AlaHanDrea vanishing like she did, Tommy decided it was time to go home ... The date was over.

He hoped beyond hope that he hadn't messed things up between them...

"AlaHanDrea, what's wrong?" Tootsie asked her frazzled friend.

"It's Tommy. We were have a great time, the best time ever, but then, he got all insistent on making a baby and I said no... More than once... I finally just vanished."

"Don't be angry at him, guys are just like that! They aren't the ones that get pregnant, so, ya, they get pushy when they get horny... It's totally a man thing!"

"I'm not sure I'm going to like adulting..." AlaHanDrea said... "Ever since I got boobs, guys have gone all weird on me ..."

"I hear ya, girlfriend."

"Tommy is one of dearest friends. Now, it's going to be weird hanging out with him, knowing that he just wants to do stuff to me.

Being all grown up just complicates things.

I do not like adulting at all!" She cried.

The world cried with her, since she forget the cameras were still on ...

Isabel noticed the broadcast was still broadcasting and concluded the broadcast for the day.

People had already gotten more than they bargained for, with the alien invasion, or, attempted alien invasion.

Witnessing the entirety of the date, to include the private conversations afterwards, played an important role for many young ladies across the globe. It helped them to put things in perspective in their own lives, as far as dating was concerned.

AlaHanDrea stopping Tommy, explaining why they couldn't make a baby... Not why they couldn't have sex, but why they couldn't make a baby... Really got through to a bunch of kids, both male and female.

Chapter 13

"Danalli, dude, I heard you're about to be a big brother and then some," Keithen commented.

"So are you! Same as me! Bray is going to be a brother again, also." Danalli added.

"Does anyone other than me find it weird that the foursome is having a bunch of babies? Well, a baby and baby dragons?" Braynar asked.

"Has a watcher ever had a baby with a human before?" Danalli asked.

"I dunno, bro," Keithen admitted.

"I sure hope they all know what the hell they are doing!" Danalli commented.

"So, does this mean we share our throne with more boys?" Keithen asked.

"Ya, I suppose it does at that," Braynar answered.

"We have weird parents," Danalli said.

Keithen and Braynar both agreed.

"So, Danalli, what's it like, being part human?"

"I don't know any other way to be. I shift the same like you do, so I doubt it's much different."

"Bray, does it feel weird being half watcher?" Keithen asked.

"I'm with Danalli, I don't know anything else. Plus, I've yet to explore my watcher side. Raynar and I are supposed to start finding out just how much watcher I really am. With a baby on the way, my uncle's may have to step in for him..."

"Sounds like it could be fun."

"I dunno, maybe. We'll see."

"So, when are any of us going to start becoming parents?" Danalli asked.

"You itching to reproduce, bro?" Keithen asked.

"I dunno. Maybe it is getting to be that time in life. We are all old enough, that's for sure." Braynar answered.

"What do you think we're waiting for, AlaHanDrea?" Danalli asked.

"I dunno, ya think that's it?" Keithen asked.

"I hadn't really thought about it, but, ya, could be!" Braynar admitted.

"Well, maybe we should all stop waiting ..." Danalli commented.

"Ya, maybe..." Braynar said.

"Hey, AlaHanDrea, are you around?"

"Braynar! Is so good to see you! What's up?"

"Well, actually, you're what's up..."

"Oh ya? How so?"

"AlaHanDrea, it's no secret that I desire you."

"No, it's no secret...."

"Do you... Do you desire me, too?"

"What's this about, Braynar?"

"Would you like to spend today with me? Do stuff together?"

"You mean, like a date?"

"Ya, I suppose you could call it a date... I would actually love the opportunity to court you..."Bray Replied.

"O.K. I believe I will love to be courted by you."

"I'm going to kiss you, you know."

"Yes, well, just know that I will kiss you back."

"O.K. just so we understand each other."

"Well, so, now what?"

"Wanna ride on my shoulder and go flying?"

"Of course I do!

Oh Braynar, you are a Magnificent Beast! Absolutely Incredible!

You take my breath away!

Just look at you!

I love it that you have a natural chair spot on your shoulder for me. I fit so nicely... O.k., I'm ready, sweet baby, lets go soar through the Heavens..."

"You really mean all of that?"

"Of course I do!"

AlaHanDrea jumped down as Braynar began to shift back to man state. He turned and looked her in the eyes...

She smiled and said," Yes, I mean every word I said."

"And as a man?"

"Braynar, as a man, you are Magnificent! Just look at you! Baby, your muscles have muscles!

You're so sculptured! Such handsome features!

Bray, you're all that and a box of rocks!"

"Well, I'm glad you approve..."

"Of course! What female would ever tell you no? And Bray, you're a prince! Not just a Prince, The Prince.

I cannot imagine any female ever telling you no! You're a hunk! And that's putting it mildly!"

"I had no idea that's how you see me,"

"Bray, you're gorgeous!"

"I'm going to kiss you... Right now. On the mouth."

"And I'm going to let you kiss me, right on the mouth... Right... Now..."

Braynar tilted her chin up with his finger, bent down and kissed her on the lips. Softly at first, then with a bit more passion, as he pulled her close, until their bodies touched.

Sparks flew! AlaHanDrea could feel electric currents surging through her body while he kissed her! She wanted more!

A fire lit deep within her... Braynar could feel her desire beginning to grow, it made his own desire grow even stronger.

He forced himself to stop, reminding himself that she was a virgin.

"Braynar, what's wrong?"

"Baby girl, you're a virgin ... there's a procedure that needs to be done first .."

"Oh, you mean, the Hymonectomy? Had that already. Then, I used a set of dilators .."

"You did?"

"Yes, but no man has been there, yet ..."

Braynar stopped holding back. She was ready and he knew he was ready!

The more they kissed and explored one another, the more energy that seemed to course through her veins... The more intense the heat of passion, the stronger the currents became, driving her wild with desire! Braynar could feel her desire, fueling his own desire, carrying them both to new heights ...

They became lost in each other and the passion building between them...

Hours passed...

Exhausted, they fell asleep in each other's arms ... Swaying in the gentle breeze, laying together in the hammock.

When the teen Queen woke up, alone in her bed, she realized it had been just a dream. A very realistic dream, but a dream nonetheless.

She took a deep breath and called out, "Braynar!"

"Hey there, baby girl, what's going on?"

"Oh Braynar, I had a dream ...... Would you please come here and hold me?"

"Well, of course I will, baby girl, everything's going to be alright, scooch over some, I'm a big guy..."

"May I please curl up on you?"

"Sweet girl, you can do anything you want on me. Do you want to talk about it? Was it a nightmare?"

"No, it was a beautiful dream, the nightmare was waking up to discover it was just a dream."

"Oh, sweet baby girl, it'll be alright. So, what was the dream about?"

"Us. You and me. It was incredible! Then I woke up... alone."

"It was about us?"

"Yes, it was and it was incredible."

Braynar raised up on an elbow, looked her in the eyes, then leaned down and kissed her. She kissed him back... He felt the desire that ached inside of her, left unfulfilled from a dream...

AlaHanDrea felt his maleness swell... She reached down to touch it, but he stopped her.

"Baby girl, you're a virgin..."

"Braynar, I'm open. I had the procedure done and have used the dilators..."

Braynar swallowed hard... He found himself to be suddenly very nervous...

"Bray, if the real thing is even partly as it was in the dream, why would you want to deny either of us such exquisite pleasure?"

He had no argument for that line of reasoning. Laying in her bed with her like that, was making it very hard to resist her. He finally asked himself why he was even trying to resist...

He began kissing her again, with a new attitude... He was determined to make certain that she enjoyed every second ... Instead of wrestling with himself over should or shouldn't ...

Braynar was top of his class in all subjects pertaining to the pleasure of females...... He was a true master...... And he made sure she could tell....

This time, she was wide awake!

Wide awake.

"Bray, baby, wow!"

"Wow?"

"Ya, wow... Bray, are you just having fun? Or... Well......"

"Damn it, Girl!

I'm in love with you!"

"I am very much in love with you, Braynar... And it's scary... We are likely to be going to have children together, and that's so o.k. with me!

Thank you for coming to me when I summoned you. I need you so much! It feels wonderful to lay with you... To be so close to another creature... It's just awesome, baby..."

"Ya, it does feel pretty good." Braynar agreed.

"It all feels pretty good! Oh, yes, it does... I don't want to stop. Bray, am I your girl?"

"Do you wanna be my girl?"

"That's a silly question! Of course I do....

What female wouldn't wanna be your girl...???

"AlaHanDrea, there's something I need to give you.... Since you are my girl... Would you like to wear my ring?"

"Braynar! It's beautiful! Yes, I'd love to wear your ring..."

"We're going to raise a family, you and I." Braynar commented.

"Ya, we are.

We're going to be someone's parents someday..."

"It could happen."

"Is it o.k. if I say, 'I Love You?'"

Chapter 14

Everyone sat up and took notice, that where ever Braynar was, so was AlaHanDrea, there, also.

The ring on her finger was hard to miss ...

Danalli & Keithen were giving Braynar a hard time about putting a ring on it...

"AlaHanDrea deserves to be able to wear a ring... Only that ring is forever hers, no matter what. It's a symbol of my love for her, always. It's forever her virgin ring. Her maidens ring.... Are you planning on stepping up, Danalli? If so, maybe you should consider also gifting her a ring..."

"Me? Has she not already chosen?" Danalli asked.

"No, she has not already chosen, Danalli. I will not ever make her choose. It just would not be right.

No, it's not going to be easy, but it's far better than living a life without enjoying being with her.

She's very much in love with Keithen, I'll not ask her to stop loving him.

AlaHanDrea is never to be possessed by anyone. She belongs to everyone, yet, belongs to no one. She's our baby girl....

She belongs to us all, the same way the trees and sky belong to us all.

It's up to us to love her, protect her, enjoy her....

Brothers, we do not compete for her. We are all three blessed to be counted among her inner circle... Tho, Keithen is standing just outside of it...

Brothers, I love you both, I would never deny you the pleasure of her."

"So, no one's going to be angry at me..." Danalli was interrupted by JayDe running as quickly as he could, so the humans that were chasing him, didn't catch him. Braynar jumped into the pathway, successfully blocking the humans from getting by...

"Your highness, Prince Braynar, sir, you don't understand! He is a menace! This werewolf!"

"Ya, he can be a tad bit of a handful at times," Braynar chuckled...

"Pardon me, your highness, but he's a bit more than a handful! He murders!"

"Well, it occurs to me that the fault lies with you. You are aware of him and his 'ways', yet you have done nothing to utilize his , uh, shall we call them, talents'?

So, find a place for him! Make him o.k. Learn to work within his perimeters... Have you tried giving him a hit list of your enemies?

Don't fear him only, a level of fear, of course, but respect him, don't just say no, so, not that, this ...

He is an alien in an alien world... Learn to work with him, turn him into an asset."

"Your highness, I bow to your intelligence and wisdom."

"Don't be a smart ass, I haven't eaten breakfast yet...

So, are you ready to meet him, socially?" Braynar asked the trembling Captain.

"Yes, your highness. In your presence and supervision, I should like very much to meet him."

"King JayDe, come on out here, little buddy, I'd like for you to meet the humans.

No biting!

Come on now, don't be shy.

This one is Captain Harrison.

Never, ever bite Captain Harrison...

At least, not without good reason...

And Captain Harrison will not ever strike against you, good reasons or no..."

"King JayDe? He's Royalty?"

The Captain asked.

"Yes, King!" Braynar stated, rather sharply.

"They want to kill me, they really wanna make me dead!," JayDe told Braynar.

"Well, today, we are going to fix this. Today, you are going to call a truce and stick to it!"

"Pardon the asking, Prince Braynar, but, uh, how are you suggesting we'll be doing that?"

"Truthfully Captain, I'm shocked he isn't in your military. You are not properly utilizing your assets, and, as a result, King JayDe, here, is left to forage...

In Addition, King JayDe is also a Shifter... Like a dragon, JayDe shifts to human form. He isn't nearly as menacing looking as a humanoid." Braynar explained to the Captain.

"Prince Braynar, I think it's only fair to tell you, that, I lose control when the moons are fully bright and visible... A hunger comes over me!

I have no control when the beast takes over.

It's not my choice to shift then... It just happens when the moons rise.

The beast takes over... "

"That's simple, when the time of the full moons comes,, you Must check in, to be placed into a comfortable, secured, home, then, fed.

Humans on death row in the prisons, would be a fun place to begin looking for suitable donations. Wouldn't you think, Captain Harrison?"

"Well, ya, yes... I suppose you're right."

"And, Captain Harrison, should you Ever feel that you have a reason to rise up against King JayDe, you will report to me at once."

Braynar gave the Captain a locket containing two buttons to push... 1 to call Braynar and one to call JayDe, for emergency use only.

"Prince Braynar, is the button strictly to be used for instances involving JayDe?" The Captain asked.

"Well, don't be abusing it, but, no, you can use it to call on me. In EMERGENCIES!"

"Yes, your highness, duly noted. And thank you, your highness!"

"I get cranky and hungry when I'm disturbed over miniscule issues, or that I see as being miniscule ... I may decide to eat you."

"Noted your highness. And... Thank You."

"The locket contains 2 buttons, Captain. One is for JayDe. When you need him, press the button. Go ahead, give it a try."

The Captain pushed the button and a communications/viewing screen appeared in the air, like the ones AlaHanDrea used.

Satisfied that the situation was then under control, Captain Harrison left, arranging a meeting with the humans in charge, to explain how JayDe was now under their employ and was on their payroll ...

'If ya can't beat em, join em!' the captain uttered under his breath...

"They wanted to kill me, Bray!

Now, I work for them!

Ha!

Now THAT'S a turn of events!"

"Do right, little buddy. I'm putting a lot of faith in you, as well as putting my power between you and your enemies, please don't make me regret it.... still, I'm making notes of your times of change.

I plan to be there by your side, holding your hands, if it comes necessary.

Embrace who and what you are. Love you, as is. Learn to work within your personal boundaries and make it o.k. for you to be you.

Take responsibility for your own actions! O.k. so what, you didn't ask for this curse. Maybe you did, maybe you didn't, that's beside the point. This is still your reality, so, find a way to make it o.k.!

Teach others how to treat you...

Whether you ask for it or not, you are still who You Are... you are still what you are and you and you alone are responsible for your actions. So, if there's a time that you cannot control yourself, pre-arrange for someone to intervene and help you. If not me, then someone, but reach out and seek help, or you have nobody to blame but your own self and I'll not interfere again.

Learn to get along...

Even with your prey.

Life becomes much more livable.

They don't mind you killing, as long as you kill those who need to be killed.

So, go be that guy.

Kill those who need it, who earned it...

Be friends with the rest."

"So, I'm the chief executioner."

"Yes, now you get it. And, they have a list of names for you to go visit, a hit list. Work with them, not against them, and you'll be much happier."

"I'm not sure I'm comfortable revealing my man state. Then, I can't hide."

"Good point. Well, ya gotta do what your comfortable with."

"Right.. right."

———

"Braynar, I hate to interrupt, but, could I please talk to you a minute?"

"Ya, uh, thanks, Bray, I was fixing to head out anyways. I'll talk to ya later. Man I'll hollar atcha in a bit..." JayDe was out before Braynar could respond, glad for that meeting to be over with.

"What's up baby girl?"

AlaHanDrea walked over to Braynar, stood in front of him, looking deep in his eyes... She gently grabbed the front of his shirt to pull him down where she could reach him to kiss him.

He put his arms around her, lifting her up for a big, passionate kiss.

AlaHanDrea, suddenly forgot everything she wanted to talk about with Braynar... They became lost in that kiss...

Braynar pinned her arms over her head in a show of dominance, then kissed her while she was pinned, for the same reason.

There was no sense trying to fight it...

He made her melt... She was like putty in his hands.

Later, as they lay, relaxing in their hammocks,

"Do you remember what it was you wanted to discuss with me?" Braynar asked...

"Yes, actually, uh yeah...

Bray, I love you so very much!

When I'm with you, being with you is all that matters to me.

You fill me with hot desire...

Nothing in this world matters, while I'm making love to you.

But, we can't be around each other 24/7. It's not healthy.

Bray, I'm wrong. Im not ready to become a mother. I'm not ready for children, Bray, I'm so sorry.

Just, not now. Do you want me to give you your ring back?"

"No, that ring is forever yours. Are you breaking up with me?"

"Well, no, uh, yes, but, uh no, not really breaking up, more like backing up. I do not want to stop seeing you. I still want to spend time with you and make love to you.

I just want to still be free.

I don't have patience for jealousy, either.

It has no room in my life.

But, I'm young. I want to experience more men before knowing who it is I wish to raise a family with.

I'd like to be free to choose more than once.

But, I don't want to lose you!

I can't lose you!

It doesn't mean I don't love you, because I so do."

"Baby girl, I completely understand.

We mean the words when we say them.

Horny makes ya crazy... Feelings come over us... Make us believe we mean the words we are saying....

And, in a sense, we do... Part of us does, anyway .. But still, it's too soon.

When you get off by yourself, you begin to realize it was horny as well as all of the emotions created during beautiful passionate loving... Doing the talking..."

That's not to say that I don't love you, because I damn sure do... I love you...

I don't want to lose you..."

"Promise me you're not going to get upset in any way..."

"Just say it, AlaHanDrea..."

"I want to go see Danalli.

I have to go see Danalli. It's a destiny thing. And I want to be free for life to happen how it happens ....

I want to love and let live...

But, I can't lose a single one of you!

Bray, why does life have to be so complicated?"

"That's a very good question, baby girl."

"I have another question for you...

Why does my own mother lie to me and why do my parents want me dead?

Could you please see to it that a full investigation is launched regarding my parents, please?

The whole thing is giving me a head ache.

I spoke to Healix, the rest of me is still in a coma from the poison."

"AlaHanDrea, what would happen if the rest of you failed to survive?"

"If the main part of me dies, all of me dies."

"Yes, baby girl, I will see to it that a full investigation happens, asap."

"Bray, may I please curl up on your lap? Will you please hold me for a moment?"

"Sure baby girl, come here, that's right, climb on up here."

"Bray, you feel so great... I could lay here indefinitely... Affection is a very good thing.

I love listening to your hear heart beat..."

"Braynar suddenly jumped to his feet, accidentally sending AlaHanDrea tumbling to the floor.

"Oh! Sweetie, I'm so sorry! I didn't mean to dump you like that, but baby girl, look here... There will none of that absorbing shit with me, got it?"

"I'm sorry sweetheart, it wasn't intentional, I swear it wasn't! I'll behave, I swear I will...."

But when she looked up, Braynar was gone... Vanished...

AlaHanDrea sat on the floor, put her face in her hand and sighed ... Then, she made visions of her play in Danalli's mind until he showed up to see her .

Braynar sent him a message, "bro, watch out for baby girl. We seem to constantly forget how deadly dangerous that girl is!

She started to absorb me! I caught her and made her stop it. I threw her on the floor. Watch yourself, bro."

"AlaHanDrea, have you been being bad" Danalli asked teasingly.

She blushed a deep crimson red... "I didn't mean to be... I was curled up on his lap and heard the beating of his heart.... and it was so soothing it joined with me... I won't let it happen again..."

"Do you not realize what you're doing when you begin absorbing a creature?"

"I don't know. Nobody ever was affectionate with me before. I'm just now learning. It just felt so good to be held in his arms and to hear the beating of his heart I was just crawling up inside of him. I should have realized what was happening myself, but I didn't."

"How do you think you would have felt when you realized what you had done and Braynar was gone?"

"Oh, but he wouldn't be gone not really. He would be a part of me forever. He would still live, just inside of me and without his own body. His body would be gone, forever a part of me also, just as food is. But his consciousness, his spirit, we live on inside of me. All that he is, would become part of me. His knowledge, his memories, his powers, his emotions... Everything that makes him him, would then be a part of me. The answer to your question, how would I feel? I don't know, it's never happened to me before. I couldn't miss him, cuz he'd be with me always. But I could miss his touch. I'm not sure these are the answers you were looking for, but I'm being honest. There would probably be moments of sadness... I don't really know, and I'm in no hurry to really find out."

"Thank you for your honesty."

"You no longer want to be with me, do you?"

"Truthfully, I honestly don't know right now."

"Danalli, understand this, had I wanted him, I would have taken him and there's not a damn thing he could have done about it. If I wanted you, I could take you right here and right now and nobody can stop me, not even you!

All y'all exist, because I say you can continue to exist and for no other reason... because, I could so take you out just wanting you gone. Please try never to forget that.

Yes, I firmly believe that I alone, could go against the entire fleet of dragon kind and come out victorious without a scratch, so don't try me, ever.

Anyway, admit it, you would love the danger of Me and You know It!"

She did have a valid point. The danger of her was intoxicating!

Her beauty was so intoxicating, that a man was willing to gladly risk his life to be with her... even if only for a moment..

"Danalli, I am who I am, and I am what I am. Love me the way I am, or leave me alone.

Enjoy me, appreciate me and all my idiosyncrasies... Or just leave me alone."

Danalli stood quietly for a moment, looking deeply into her eyes, then went over to her, pulled her close, kissing her a kiss that made them both feel lost in love... Connected...

"Baby girl, I have waited so, so long for this moment! This time, it's really you! I loved you the moment I set eyes on you, but I've wanted you badly, yearned for you, since our time in the field of flowers...

Finally, you body has grown old enough......

This time, these moments, oh my sweet baby girl..." He said, then kissed her again....

Chapter

Chapter 15

"Damn... That woman is gorgeous! Who is she?" Donald asked his brother, Jimmy. It was their first day on Taurus 9, out of quarantine.

Jason, of the royal guard said, " that woman is Queen AlaHanDrea."

"She's so young to be a queen," Donald remarked

"She is extremely powerful. She also eats creatures like you." Jason added.

"You mean figuratively eats...."

"No, I mean, consumes your body as nourishment for hers." Jason explained.

"She's a cannibal?" Jimmy asked.

"No, she's not human," Jason explained.

"Oh!" They both said at the same time.

"Anyway, if you wanted to get close to her, you see those 2 dragons over there, wearing crowns on their heads? You'd have to go through them to get to her." Jason told them.

"Oh." They both said, together, again.

AlaHanDrea could hear every word they were saying and was feeling playful ... As well as a bit ornery!

She walked over to them, looking as sexy as she knew how to be... She could feel the desire rising in all 3, the two aliens And Jason! She loved the effect she had on males, of all species...

"Hello, Jason, so, who are your friends?" She asked.

"Your majesty, this is Jimmy and his brother, Donald."

"Very nice to meet you both. Uh, Jason, I have a little gift for you."

"For me, your majesty?" Jason asked, surprised.

"Yes." She used her magic to produce a Brandy glass. She pulled her fangs out and placed the glass behind them and pressed her venom sacks, allowing droplets of her venom to drip down the sides of the glass. She put a tight seal over the glass and handed it to Jason. "Now, Jason, be extremely careful with my venom. Any contact and you die instantly. Guard this. Put it up somewhere safe.

Go ahead, you can go do it now, I will gladly look after your 2 friends..." She joked.

Jason caught on right away and decided to play along.

"Well okay, I suppose it'll be alright. I'm supposed to be watching after them to make sure that they don't get themselves into any kind of trouble while they get settled. Your majesty, have you eaten today?"

"Yes, but to tell you the truth, it wasn't really very filling. But that's all right, you can go right on ahead and go take care of that venom and I'll watch your two friends." She joked.

"Well, okay. I suppose that'll be all right. I'd hate to get in trouble with the King. After all, he did tell me to watch after these guys... make sure that no harm came to them... Of course, there are none more powerful than you, your majesty.

I'm sure they'll be okay in your care... Won't they be?"

"Oh, well of course they will. They'll be just fine. And should I decide to taste one of them, I promise to only take the one," she joked.

"Well okay then. Having one left will be better than not having any left," he joked before taking off.

The two men had terror stricken faces!

AlaHanDrea asked them, "what do y'all say we play a little game? A what if game... Each one of you, tell me why the other one should be spared. Jimmy, you go first."

"Spared, your majesty?"

"Yes, tell me why I should not eat him. If you can convince me to not eat him, then he is spared. However, if you do not convince me, then I will eat him. If neither one of you can convince me to not eat the other one, then I will eat you both.

Sing his praises as though his life depends on it," she instructed.

The two men sat silently for a moment. Jimmy couldn't help but to think how cruel it was to make him convince her not to eat Donald when that left him to be eaten... He didn't want Donald to get eaten, but more than that, he didn't want to get eaten. Still, she said he was to convince her that Donald should not be supper. Jimmy began by telling her what a good heart Donald had. He told her how Donald took care of those who couldn't take care of themselves. He spoke of how his brother taught his students and how all of his students loved him. He spoke of Donald's talents as well as his generous spirit. He spoke of Donald's community work and his sense of community...

AlaHanDrea said, "okay, but none of that means anything to me. In order for that to mean something to me, I would have to care about your communities.

Jimmy talked and talked, finally, AlaHanDrea told his brother to give it a try.

Donald thought hard, then said, "your majesty, you should not eat Jimmy. His diet consists of greasy food that would be bad for your beautiful complexion. He eats very hot and spicy food as well and he would most likely give you a bad case of indigestion. He's skinny and would not be very filling. With the amount of dairy he eats daily, he would probably constipate you as well. In addition, I wouldn't think he would taste very good. He often has a sour attitude that I would assume, makes his meat taste terrible! Anyway, you'd just be hungry again in an hour. Also, King George's instructions were to make sure no harm would come to us. Eating jimmy could possible upset his majesty and I wouldn't want that man mad at you over a poor lunch like Jimmy."

"Well, you make some very good points there, now, Donald. What about you? Is your diet as bad as Jimmy's?" She asked, further teasing Donald.

Reluctantly he said, "no. I have a great diet. Now, I'm suddenly wishing that I didn't."

"O.k., so, you did your very best to save your brother, believing that I would eat you in his place?"

"Yes. And... I'm ready. If I must be eaten, at least it's by someone as gorgeous as you! You are truly beautiful and I'm Not just saying that, either!"

"Donald, you can both relax. And, thank you...

I wasn't going to eat either of you.

I was playing with you!

I hope you can see the humor and not be too upset with me...you must admit, it was kind of funny, don't you think?" She asked, giggling.

Both men cracked up laughing. "You really had us going!" Jimmy said.

"Excuse me, your majesty, I don't mean to interrupt, but your lunch is here," Craigen told her.

"Oh, o.k. Just bring it in, I'll eat right here," she instructed him.

"As you wish," Craigen told her as he rolled the food wagon in.

The two brothers stared in disbelief at the food wagon containing humans. They had thought she was kidding about eating humans when she said she was messing with them about choosing to eat one of them. They watched in horror while she consumed three full grown men before an eye could be batted. Then, she burped and said, " Scuse me!" And giggled, as usual.

Braynar went over to the small group, "excuse me, I enjoyed watching that! AlaHanDrea, did you not think that Jimmy's arguments were made with him believing he would be eaten instead?"

"Sorta. You see, Jimmy knew he had to at least appear to be trying to save his brother, so, he made a point to sound as convincing as possible, by pointing out his character traits... Donald here, truly wanted to save his brother. He heard my criticism and after giving it some thought, he realized he had to say things that I'd actually care about. He told me why Jimmy would be bad for me, as a meal. He knew that would get to me.

Somewhere in Jimmy's mind, he had to know that I don't give 2 hoots and a holler about aliens I don't know. He simply made it appear as tho he truly cared about his brother, all the while, secretly hoping I'd choose his brother and not him.

Not once did he actually plead for his brothers life, or, try to make deals with me to let them both go... He believed I'd eat him if he was too convincing...

He simply pointed out what a good guy his brother is.

Donald won this competition.

I should like for Donald's home to be built very near my own, please. I like him. "

"As you wish, your majesty."

"You don't mind living in a beast community, do you Donald?" AlaHanDrea asked him.

"Not at all, your majesty!"

"Good. Your brother will remain with the humans. I'm sorry, but I don't trust him and neither should you. Worry not, there are humans in our community, as well. Not many, but a few."

"I understand... I'm not sure I agree, but I do understand. I mean, he is my brother...

Is there someplace for me to get a job near there?"

"No, why would you want to get a job?"

"Do I not need one?"

"You have no time for one. You already have one.... I need you to be available when I need you to be available and not off on some weird job."

"Oh! O.k., my apologies, your majesty.

"You will report to Queen Tootsie. She is in charge over the orphans project. She will place you where you'll be best served...."

"The orphan project? "

"Yes, we are building a community based on the caring for orphans, mostly human orphans. I believe I heard you volunteer?"

"Thank you, yes, you did hear me volunteer!

What an awesome project! That's quite an undertaking, your majesty. I'll do my best to help in anyway I can."

"Why were you chosen for the colonization program that brought you to Taurus 9?"

"I'm a carpenter, your majesty. A contractor I build neighborhoods," he explained. Before becoming a Contractor, I was a school teacher."

"I knew you'd be great for this!! Donald, come to my home in 30 minutes." She whispered, then vanished.

Braynar was shocked she vanished. "Now, where did she go? Oh well, I'll ask her later."

"Can someone please show me to the site of my new home?" Donald asked.

Jason volunteered and showed him to the area of AlaHanDrea's home, then left.

"Donald, glad to see that you could make it. Would you like to come up and see my home?"

"Sure!" He exclaimed.

"You have a very impressive tree house, your majesty. "

"Thank you." She said.

"Your majesty, may I please kiss you." He asked.

"Why would you want to do that?" She asked him.

"Truthfully, I'd like to do a bit more than that, but I'll be happy to start with a kiss. I'm sorry, was that not why you asked me to your home? I'm so sorry! I thought... Well....."

"Oh, you're horny.

Well, I'm not here for that. I'm a queen.

A warrior queen.

I also have very high standards, no offense.

I have just recently come of age and have limited experience, however, my experience has been with masters, so far.

I'm not sure your kind even has classes available."

"Classes?"

"Yes, dragons have a college for their adolescent males.

They go see Lord Pooky the Love Dragon for a couple of years.

They are taught all about the art of pleasing females.

That's one of the reasons for the lack of wars on this planet.... We have them, just not very many and not very often.

"Wow, that's really incredible! I'm a dragon, too, you know."

"You are part dragon, yes, I see it in you. Your brother must be adopted, because he has no dragon in Him at all. He's all human."

"Are you sure, your majesty?"

"Of course I'm sure. He's all human. Is he older or younger than you?"

"He is younger than me."

"Then, y'all don't have the same two parents. He's not a dragon."

"I never knew that. It does explain a few things, though."

Can you/will you, shift for me. You can get on the ground first, if ya like."

"I'm afraid that I don't know how to shift, your majesty."

She took his hand and a moment later, they were on the ground. "Here, hold both of my hands and let your mind go. Do not resist me!" She instructed. He started to try to free his hands, then yelled out as he began to shift! She stood looking at him. He was the strangest looking dragon she'd ever seen!

He was a dragon, but shaped like a man, with wings. She produced a full length mirror for him to see himself.

He was shocked!

Braynar came walking up to them. "Well, there you are, brethren!

Let's have a look at you! Well, alrighty then! AlaHanDrea, thank you so much!

If you don't mind, I'm going to take charge of this one for a bit. Thank you so much for helping him!"

"You boys go have fun!

I'll see ya both soon, but Braynar, aren't you forgetting something?" She asked with a sexy smile.

"Oh, my bad!" He said, then walked over to her, lifted her up and kissed her with passion. Heat began to rise in them both! She wrapped her legs around him and whispered in his ear, " I love you, Bray!" Then she hopped down and smiled.

Braynar had a big ol smile on his face. He winked at her then left with Donald.

When ALaHanDrea turned back around, a very large man was standing there. She'd never even seen this one before!

He grabbed her around the waist and put his hand over her mouth. She decided to play along, even though she could kill him with almost no effort at all.

She squirmed to remain convincing.

"Stop your squirming or I'll kill you!

Make a sound, and I will kill you, understand?" He said, as he slowly took his hand away from her mouth.

"what do you want?" She asked the man.

"Isn't that obvious? I want you to get naked and spread those legs for me."

"Now, why in the world would I want to be doing a thing like that for?" She asked, playing dumb.

"Because if you don't, I will kill you!" He barked.

She took a step back, unfastening her top, slowly, letting the girls out, slowly. Then, she unbuttoned her bottoms, slowly, while she was ever so slowly pulling down her pants, she told him to get naked too!

Once he exposed himself, she looked at his penis and began laughing! Then she laughed harder, pointing at it and said, "that's your penis? No wonder you have to force women to have sex with you! Then she laughed even harder. The man was infuriated! He reached out for her, but she vanished! Then reappeared behind him. This went on for a few minutes, then Danalli showed up....

Danalli grabbed the man by his throat and held the man with his toes barely touching the ground.

AlaHanDrea explained to Danalli what was happening. Then she told him that death was too good for this man, he should be enslaved to the mines inside of the mountain for as long as he managed to survive. The guy was choking & beginning to turn blue! Danalli agreed with AlaHanDrea and had him taken below to the mines.... his earning were for his victims...

"Danalli, why do human males choose to steal sex from females?"

"actually, it isn't limited to human males, sweetheart."

"Ya, that's true. O.k., so, why do some males take sex instead of earning it by convincing the females to do it?"

"I don't know, Let's perform a little experiment," he said, then grabbed her, pinning her where she couldn't move. He threw her over his shoulder and carried her like a sack of potatoes, into a nearby cave. He used his magic to quickly furnish the cave and put her down on the bed he created, (more like dropped her), then climbed on top of her, restraining her hands. "Danalli, that's enough, you can stop now."

He ignored her. He sat up and ripped her top off of her, then restrained her ankles.

"Danalli, what are you doing? I said no! I want you to stop!" He continued to ignore her...

"Damn, you are so incredibly beautiful!" he said, as he stood, gazing down at her.

He sat next to her on the bed, "well, did it turn you on? Because it actually did kinda turn me on. But then, I love you and this was a controlled situation with trust involved." Danalli said.

"You know I'd never do anything to hurt you."

"I know you wouldn't. I was a little scared, but now, I find myself wishing you'd do stuff....."

"Oh yeah? Well.... Hmm, what kind of stuff?" He asked teasingly, then kissed her with red hot passion.

They discovered each other in many ways that night.... Early the next morning, AlaHanDrea woke up, laying in Danalli's arms. He felt her stir and woke up. "Good morning, gorgeous!"

"Good Morning, sweet baby. This is very nice!"

"Yes, it is!" He said, then showed her just how good of a morning it could be.

Before they realized it, the noon horn was blowing....

"I don't know about you, but I'm hungry," Danalli said to AlaHanDrea.

"Let's go hunting, Danalli."

"Sure, sounds good to me!"

"But first, I'm going for a quick swim..."

"Right behind you," he teased, swatting her bottom.

After their swim, AlaHanDrea climbed up on Danalli's shoulder for their hunting trip.

One of AlaHanDrea's favorite things was riding on Danalli.

She really missed it while she was on mimic island.

Their hunting was going really slowly, when they spotted a group of people on the ground that seemed to have captured a bunch of unicorns!

AlaHanDrea was furious! She jumped up on her feet in attack position. Danalli swooped down, scooping up 2 people in his talons and one in his mouth. AlaHanDrea snatched the female out of

Danalli's talon and drug her up onto his shoulder, cocooning her and attaching her to Danalli's mane.

"Who are you and what are you doing with My Unicorns???" AlaHanDrea demanded

"They aren't just your unicorns!" The girl smart mouthed.

"They damned sure are, My Unicorns! And! I brought them here from my home planet, well, moon. Now, who the hell are you?"

"We are just people. We want the horses for our ranch."

"Those Horses are Unicorns."

"Ya, you already said that."

"You have no right to take them!" AlaHanDrea said very sternly.

"Excuse me, I have every right! They carry no brand!" The stupid girl insisted.

Danalli headed for the ground and landed. AlaHanDrea jumped down and began throwing cocoons around people and making others freeze like statues.

The upset teen queen used her magic to free her friends.

"Please, shift for me," she asked her friends.

"Danalli, please bring the stupid smart mouthed girl over here. You see these people? You still think you have a right?"

"They're people?!? Wow! We didn't know! They are so beautiful! We wanted them for our ranch. Every since we got the first ones..."

"What do you mean, the first ones? Where is this ranch?"

Danalli and AlaHanDrea headed for the ranch as quickly as they could.

As they approached the ground, they spotted a unicorn about to be killed!

Danalli swooped down, blowing flames at the human aiming a weapon at the beautiful beast, setting him ablaze!

AlaHanDrea used her magic to open every door and gate on the property, setting the unicorns free!

Well over 100 unicorns took off running for home.

Danalli circled around and began blowing flames until every structure on the ranch was on fire! It was the best way he knew to keep the humans from chasing down the escapees...

And, it worked!

Furious at all they had just experienced, they headed back to more familiar surroundings.

No sooner had the weary warriors landed, than the fairies rushed over to greet them.

It seemed the humans were broadcasting a story saying that Danalli and AlaHanDrea attacked a ranch without warning or provocation of any kind.

They were showing video footage of the burning buildings....

AlaHanDrea was even more furious than before!

She brought up a viewing screen at once.

"Please pardon the interruption, Queen AlaHanDrea here.

You're only getting a fraction of the story.

Please, allow me to fill in the blanks.

These creatures right here are not horses... they are unicorns and are not native to this world.

I brought them with me when I moved here!

They are MY Creatures!

Poachers were illegally rounding them up and when we arrived at that ranch, they were about to murder one, just to see what she tastes like and to have her horn!

They had stolen well over 100 of my Unicorns and we set them free!

No one is to ever lay a hand on one of My Unicorns!

To do so is an act of war!

I will not repeat myself.

Good day."

Chapter 16

The sound of rhythm drums filled the air, signaling the coming of the night.

The voices of male dragons joined the beat of the drums. Stringed instruments joined in, as did some woodwinds....

AlaHanDrea knew in an instant those were the voices of Braynar, Keithen and Danalli. They sang of a brothers love for a brother...

They sang of a love they could never possess, but would cherish until the end of time ...

It brought tears to AlaHanDrea's eyes...

She loved them, dearly.

She was still pretty angry at Keithen, but she loved him just the same.

As she listened to him sing, her heart ached for him. She had always thought they would be together forever...

It broke her heart that they meant more to her than she did to them.

"AlaHanDrea, are you alright?

Well no, you're not alright! You've been crying! Oh sweet girl, what troubles you?

Who has hurt you to tears?"

Kenneth asked her.

Oh! Kenneth! Hello, I'm sorry, I didn't hear you come up."

"I just wanted to check on you.

We haven't really had a chance to visit since you've been home.

When you were a kid, we visited pretty much every day!"

"I'm so sorry, I suppose we haven't. You mean, I pestered you pretty much every day..." She joked.

"Oh Kenneth, why does life and love have to be so hard?"

"Ah! Growing pains, I should have known..."

"It's not fair, Kenneth!

I love all of my dragons...

All of my friends...

All my creatures...

I don't want to pick and choose....

I don't want limits or rules that say who I can and cannot love... Or how many I can love... It's just not fair!"

"I whole heartily agree. It's your life, your rules... Change them .."

"Is it really as simple as all that?"

"Na, if only it were..."

"Ya..."

"AlaHanDrea, I have a confession to make. I'm ashamed of myself.

You see, when the mimic was here, well, I was with her.

I thought I was with you.

I should have known it wasn't you.

I mean, she didn't hesitate to be with me."

"Kenneth! Now, why wouldn't I react just like she did?

You are an incredible dragon! And... An even more incredible man, if that's even possible! You are absolutely magnificent as both, man and dragon!

You're a very fierce warrior. You fight by my side... You've fought next to me since I was just a small child! I adore you, Kenneth!"

"You do?"

"Yes, Kenneth, I do. I used to have the biggest crush on you!"

"You did?"

"Yes, I did. I still do, truth be told.

You're amazing! absolutely amazing!

There's no one I'd rather see beside me in battle!

When I see you there, I know everything's going to be alright!

As long as your there, well, I always know that you've got my back!

And, I've got yours!

Come here Kenneth, may I please have a hug?

I seriously need one.

I just need to be held for a minute..."

"Of course."

"You're so tall! Here, let me stand on this rock, there, now, that's much better... "

The hug felt really good to her in her emotional state, but she hadn't expected to feel electricity between them!

He pulled back from the hug, gazing deeply into her eyes, then leaned in for a kiss.

He kissed her ever so gently at first.

Sparks flew!

When she didn't resist, he held her closer and kissed her with more passion.

He took her breath away!

She couldn't believe how Kenneth made her feel!

"AlaHanDrea, my queen, I love you with my whole heart." He took her hand in his and slipped a ring onto her first finger.

"This ring is for you, always. It's a reminder of my never ending love for you and devotion to you

It's not an ownership ring, it's a symbol of my love for you.

Please accept it and wear it always."

"Oh Kenneth, it's gorgeous! Yes, I will gladly wear it, always!

It's just beautiful!

Thank you!"

"AlaHanDrea, I need you now." He said, then kissed her with more passion and a sense of urgency, then, scooped her up in his arms, rolled out his wings and flew to his lair.

As soon as he landed, he used his magic to light his fireplaces and put on music, still holding her in his arms.

She had her arms around his neck as well. He kissed her again, before putting her down.

It excited him that she was kissing him back!

AlaHanDrea hadn't expected all of that! Kenneth took her by surprise, but she wasn't objecting.

"My queen, my beautiful queen ... I want you so much! I need to feel you so badly... Please, be mine, even if for only a little while." He said, then began getting very familiar with her...

She honestly didn't know how to react. She wasn't expecting any of it and wasn't real sure what to make of it all!

But, she didn't resist.

She allowed things to just happen as they happened.

Kenneth was a very aggressive dragon and just as aggressive of a man... He was used to taking what he wanted!

But, it was AlaHanDrea that initiated things as far as they went!

She gently pushed him down into his big chair and sat on his lap, facing him! However, they remained clothed, the farthest they went was making out.

Kenneth actually behaved himself.

They enjoyed the intimate affection of their moments....

Kenneth surprised himself that day....

He restrained himself from taking advantage of her vulnerable state.

Very unlike him...

About 45 minutes later, she sat with her head still resting on his shoulder, his arms around her, still holding her close.

As much as she didn't want to, she finally climbed down off of his lap.

"AlaHanDrea, I'm not trying to own you or change your life, I'm good with stolen moments... I'm so good with keeping us between us. It's less complicated when us guys are together."

"I believe I can understand that.

So, how am I getting home?"

"I'm taking you back. The guys are probably still by the fire singing.

Anyway, so what if they see me returning you. We went for a fly around.... It's not the first time you and I took off for a fly around... When you were still a youngster, I used to fly you around a bunch!

Quite frankly, what you and I do or don't do is really none of anyone else's damned business."

"Ya, that's true enough."

The flight back was exhilarating.

The intimate time spent with Kenneth, sharing effecting, was just what the distraught young queen needed.

She was far more relaxed on the flight back, than she was when Kenneth first found her.

She was glad they had that time together. Glad that Kenneth was able to unburden himself.

As they soared through the air, AlaHanDrea couldn't help but to notice the way the amethyst in her new ring, caught the moonlight, making it sparkle like a distant star.

Kenneth was correct!

The guys were still singing by the fire.

Reluctantly, he left AlaHanDrea off by her place and took to the air.... Smiling.....

AlaHanDrea climbed into her hanging wicker teardrop chair to enjoy swinging in the gentle breeze, while listening to the sound of the dragons singing....

She sat there, rocking in the breeze.

It seemed so natural to sing along with the man dragons that had her heart....

She hadn't noticed the absence of one of the voices....

She was singing along, not really paying attention, until she felt her chair stop.

It was being held by somebody, standing behind her...

"I know you're mad at me, and, I really don't blame you. You have no reason to believe me, but AlaHanDrea, I honestly do love you, girl.

Think what you will, but your my best friend, girl!

We sometimes don't really realize how much someone truly means to us.... Until we blow it with them...

Oh, I so badly wish that I could turn back time! I wish so Badly that I could take back the things I've done....

There was a time I thought we'd be married... you and I... I can't imagine my life without you in it!

I hope the day comes that you find it in your heart to forgive me, and you love me again.... I miss you, AlaHanDrea! I miss us and yes, I do want to make love to you! Me and every other male in the world.

I love you and I miss you....." then, her swing swung freely in the breeze again.

Just like that, he was gone.

He had said what he came to say, and was gone.... A few moments later, she could once again hear his voice joining with the voices of his brothers....

He sang of heart break and mistakes....

Lost loves...

AlaHanDrea began singing with more volume, so that her voice could be heard along with the voices of the men....

She got up and slowly walked to the fire, singing along the way.....

she sang of love, mistakes and forgiveness....

Of new beginnings...

then switched gears and began singing comedy between the verses sung by the men... such beautiful Melodie's with the funniest lyrics!

She absolutely loved heckling the men thru song..... they'd do their best not to laugh while continuing to sing seriously....

All of guys were smiling as she entered the area.

Danalli grabbed ahold of her and added dance to the singing!

All three men began dancing with her while singing.

They'd spin her, toss her between them, doing all kinds of acrobatic stunts with her....

Danalli tossed her in the air, but it was Keithen that caught her. He lowered her slowly, facing him, paused when she was eye level, gazing into her eyes, "I miss you!" Then, he set her down and gave her a twirl. Braynar caught her when she stopped twirling around.

A larger crowd gathered, as the 4 of them sang and danced, having a great time together....

Then, another voice could be heard approaching, singing his way into the fire area.... It was Leon! Braynar picked her up, tossed her into the air, but it was Leon that caught her!

She did a one handed handstand on Leon's hand, did the splits while doing a one handed handstand on one of Leon's hands, then Leon tossed her back into the air, caught her and rolled her down, catching her by a hand and a foot before she hit the ground.... spinning her around before setting her back on her feet.

They were all really enjoying themselves.

After that song ended,

Braynar began singing beautiful lyrics, solo... He had such a deep, booming voice, he could stir up emotions in anyone!

AlaHanDrea stepped up and began singing duet with him. Their voices complimented each other very well!

Danalli decided things were getting too serious again, so he took over the role of singing heckler... Then Keithen and Leon joined

Danalli singing lyrics that had listeners about to pee themselves from laughing so hard....

It was obvious to everyone that all 4 men truly loved the teen queen... And that she loved them back!

What none of them had realized, was that the camera drones were flying over head, broadcasting ...

Finally, the roar of applause and the deafening sound of cheers gave the secret away!

All five laughed when they saw them!

In light of recent events, it was good for humanity to see them enjoying their night ... They weren't upset even a little bitty bit.

All five of them believed it was imperative they keep a good fan base in the human sector.

They weren't wrong!

One of the most trending topics among the humans, was which man AlaHanDrea would end up choosing, not realizing that her men loved her too much to ever make her choose.

Leon sure got a lot of votes!

Leon and Danalli held the lead, then Braynar, then Dane and finally Keithen tied for last place with Tommy. A few votes went to George, Isabel, Raynar and Barbara...

A few votes even went to Bob!

King Neptune even received a hand full of votes, though it was rumored that he instigated them...

Surprisingly, Craigen received a few hundred write in votes!...

There was actually a line of suitor wannabees... Johann, Peoarin, Frederick, and many more.

Nectar was flowing pretty freely, when a large pool appeared, with the water bubbling and churning.... AlaHaNdrea got super excited! Athena was coming!

Ground fog announced Mitchins arrival at about the same time.

Mitchin walked up to the fire saying, "yes, I'm an angel, but I'm a vacationing angel. Who wants to help me break a few commandments, commit a few sins???" He shouted.

The crowd went wild!

A sexy voice cut through the noise, "I'd be happy to help you break a commandment or 3!" Athena winked at him with that smile of hers that lit up any room she was in!

Applause rose up for Athena.

Everyone Loved Athena and her band of mermaids....

(The humans of Taurus 9 we're just discovering the mer population).

Poles went up very quickly... more drums showed up!

At least a dozen mermaids were there.

6 of them, in their drylander mode, climbed up on the poles and began showing off their incredible skills.

The other half a dozen were all over the Dragons...

Leon grabbed ahold of AlaHanDrea's hand and led her away from the crowds, while no one was looking.

No one but a camera drone, that is....

AlaHanDrea had drank quite a bit of nectar and was feeling no pain!

The music was great, the nectar was flowing, the night was still young and the company couldn't have been any better....

Leon had drank quite a bit his own self.

They were both feeling pretty good. Leon took AlaHanDrea in his strong arms and began dancing with her under the light of the moons...the dancing was heating the tipsy couple up, lighting fires deep inside of them both.

Leon wasn't sure how much longer he could hold off... he began to think he should leave while he still could... only it was already too late. A team of wild horses couldn't have drug him away from her!

Every second that passed, brought them closer together.

The dancing became seductive and passionate.

AlaHanDrea did a spectacular acrobatic move, Leon caught her, lowering her slowly, facing him, then he kissed her and forgot all about dancing!

Desire for her was all that existed in that moment.

Every female watching wished they were her! Leon was quite the desirable bachelor!

AlaHanDrea's knees went weak during that kiss, as a fire began to burn inside of her. Leon used his magic to create a quick hut, lightly furnished, then scooped her up and carried her Inside, laying her down on a hammock and climbing in beside her.

They looked into each other's eyes again, both of them were flooded with emotions and desire.

Leon softly kissed her lips, then began to advance, when AlaHanDrea surprised him and stopped him. He'd try to touch her while kissing her and she'd push his hand away.

Finally, he stopped, leaned up and looked at her again... "baby, what's wrong? I thought this was what we both wanted?"

"Oh Leon, it is, but, it isn't. I mean, yes, I do want you, but no, I don't think this is a good time or place. For one thing, I don't want to be drunk. I mean, I don't want to make the decision while drunk. If my mind is already made up, then being drunk is fine, but, decisions made while drunk are often poor decisions.... I never want being with you to be a poor decision.

Leon, I love you and I adore you!

Did you know that I remember the first time I saw your mom and dad? I was just born by a couple of days, not even a full 3 days. You were just a cub. And what a cute cub you were, too!

I remember looking at you and thinking to myself, that you and I would be together always.... That you'd forever be a part of my life, an important part....

I remember when you went through your 'eeew girls' stage.... Yet, you'd still smile when you looked at me...

I don't want to mess us up. You're too important to me... to important to the rest of my life."

"Well, ok then," he said, as he got up out of the hammock. He straightened his clothes and turned to leave. "Leon, where are you going?"

"Hey, I'm not pushing myself on anyone. I know when I'm not wanted," he said as he turned and walked out, causing the hut to vanish, leaving AlaHanDrea sitting on the ground without a hammock.

"Leon..."

But he didn't even look back, he just walked away without another word.

"Oh Leon..." she said out loud, frustrated.

She got up and turned around and he was standing there. "You called my name? Change your mind?"

"Leon, please, don't be mad at me."

"I'll take that as a no," he said and this time, he vanished.

AlaHanDrea had never seen him use magic to make himself vanish before.

He must have truly been upset with her, was what she was thinking.

"Men!" She said out loud, then saw the drone!

She hadn't noticed the drone had followed them before that moment.

That drone meant that everyone had just seen Leon get rejected! "Oh no!" Is all she said, out loud.

The drone pilot had a tendency to record for later broadcast when he saw thing may get inappropriate for general audiences.

As much as the pilot secretly loved AlaHanDrea, he recorded but did not broadcast, from the moment Leon forgot about dancing.

AlaHanDrea didn't know that, though. She thought the whole world just witnessed him being rejected.

Much to her surprise, a viewing screen popped up.

There must have been multiple drones, because one of them managed to attach itself to Leon!

She saw him on the viewing screen and it didn't look good, at all!

The drone pilots were really good to have managed to follow Leon with magic involved!

Much to AlaHanDrea's surprise, Leon was in lion state and was in a Cage!

She looked up at the drone watching her, "hey, can you take me to where Leon is? Or, can you show me where Leon is?"

Leon's location came up on the viewing screen! AlaHanDrea ran back to the fire where the guys were still taking turns singing.

When the guys saw her, they stopped... they could tell something was bad wrong.

"Braynar, Leon's in Trouble!

Someone has him locked up in a cage!

They used magic to get him!"

The viewing screen popped up, showing Leon's location.

The look on the guys faces was not good!

They actually looked scared!

"Bray, Danalli, what's wrong?"

"I'll go get King Leon," Keithen said as he hurried off to go get the big kitties dad...

"Dad!" Braynar and Danalli shouted at the same time. AlaHanDrea was confused as well as scared half out of her mind for Leon.

"Danalli, please y'all need to tell me what's going on!" AlaHanDrea insisted.

Braynar shouted, "Raynar! Jax! Come now!" He had such an urgency in his voice! AlaHanDrea was beginning to panic!

George, Raynar, King Leon and Jax all arrived at about the same time. Danalli and Braynar began filling them in. The look on their faces wasn't good!

"Would someone please...."

"AlaHanDrea, come with me a moment," Danalli told her, leading her over to Braynar's Lair. She was so trusting, she just followed him.

They got to the lair, but Danalli was taking her further into the mountain!

She had never been down deep before.

She knew the mines were down there and had no desire to go anywhere near the mines.

Not to mention the fact that the ore in some of the mountains, had a way of blocking magical abilities.

"Danalli, where are you taking me?"

He stopped, turned to her and said, "oh, I'm sorry sweetheart, I just wanted to get somewhere we wouldn't be overheard or disturbed."

"O.k. this is actually a nice room, I love the furnishings, what's this room used for?"

"You worry too much," he said, then pulled her close, holding her firmly. "Girl, you are so beautiful!" He said then kissed her.

Even as worried as she was, she couldn't help but to respond to Danalli. He could make her forget anything, including her own name!

Suddenly, she felt the cold of steel snapping around her wrists and began to feel lightheaded, almost faint.

Danalli picked her up and carried her over to the bed, attached the handcuffs he had put on her to the wall and secured her ankles.

"Danalli, what's going on? Danalli, I feel so strange, did you drug me? Did you.........." She passed out.

"Danalli, bro, are you going to stay down here with her?" Braynar asked. He was standing in the entry way of the area. "The rest of us are going to try to contact the counsel of wizards and see why they have taken Leon. What ever you do, don't let her get up!"

" Ya, I'll go ahead and stay. Someone has to. May as well be me. Bray, should we make her forget for now?"

"Great idea, I'll do it," Braynar said, then stepped over and hid her memories from her for awhile.

"Thanks bro. I may as well unchain her now. Are you going to close the cage door?" Danalli asked.

Ya, but I'm not going to lock it. You can, that way, you have the key." Braynar told him.

"Good luck, bro. Please stay away from the Echneumons! And don't be pissing off any wizards!" Danalli told his brother as Braynar walked off, waving at him over his shoulder as he walked away.

Danalli took the chains off of AlaHanDrea and used his magic to redecorate the cage they were locked in, before the drugs wore off and she woke up.

"Danalli, where are we, what happened? Oh! my head!"

"Well, hello there, sleepyhead! Don't you remember?"

"If I remembered, I wouldn't be asking you!"

"Well, ya, that's true enough. Here, drink this, it will help with your headache."

"Thanks. Now, please, what happened, what's going on, where are we and why are we here?"

"O.k. well, what happened, is that we were all dancing together, you, me, Leon, Braynar and Keithen, and we had an accident. You fell pretty hard and hit your head.

We are deep inside of a cave, hiding because there are some upset wizards trying to hunt us down over the unicorns. It's best we just hide, otherwise, we will have to end them and we don't want to do that.

George, Jax, Raynar and King Leon have gone to try to fix things. Until then, you and I are staying down here, where it's safe."

"But, we are in a cage..."

"Yes, that we are. And for good reason. We don't want you going all super protector. Beings will die."

"So, you and I are caged?"

"No, actually, you're caged, I'm keeping you company." Danalli was wondering why he was unable to lie past the initial lie he told her. He wasn't going to tell her any of that! Oh well, at least she was unaware that Leon was in trouble, was what Danalli was thinking...

"I'm caged.

Y'all threw me in a cage... I take it you also bound my powers?

You left out the part about Leon being captured and I did not hit my head, you drugged me!

Damnit, all y'all totally underestimate my powers!

You think you're powerful enough, that Braynar is powerful enough, to bind MY Powers?

Are you nuts?

Y'all are delusional!

You think you have ME locked in?" AlaHanDrea blew the door of the cage into little pieces.

"What made y'all think for one minute that you are powerful enough to control me on any level?

Y'all are nuts!"

"AlaHanDrea, please... I'm sorry for lying to you, or trying to lie to you! We just don't want you involved, not yet."

"Well, too damned bad!"

"George, Jax, Raynar, King Leon! Appear before me, NOW!!!" She shouted.

"Braynar, Keithen, appear before me NOW!" She demanded.

All of them appeared, trying to talk at the same time.

"Shut...Up!" She told them.

She made a screen appear.

"This is QUEEN ALAHANDREA AND I'M PISSED OFF! RETURN PRINCE LEON, UNHARMED AND RETURN HIM AT ONCE, OR THE DESTRUCTION BEGINS!!!" She shouted as the ground began to tremble.

"Raynar, who has Leon," she demanded.

"Merrill, of wizards keep,"

Raynar replied, unable to lie and upset that she was overpowering him.

"Why has Merrill captured Leon?"

"He wants to trade Leon for the unicorn called Lisa..." Raynar told her.

"And just what does this wizard want with Lisa?"

He wants her for her magic. He wants to own her."

"No one can own a Unicorn! No one! They are MINE! And as Mine, they will always run free! I will NOT be bullied into giving Lisa to him!"

"AlaHanDrea, Merrill will kill my son! Please!"

"No! And No, Leon will NOT be harmed!

As soon as I get Leon back, we are ALL going to have a long talk!

Trying to over power ME!

Trying to bind MY power and Lock ME on a cage!

Y'all have lost your minds!

All y'all!!!

Every last ONE OF YOU!" She yelled, then vanished.

They turned to leave, but the gate was intact on the cage... and locked!

"She LOCKED Us In??? She locked us in!" George shouted.

"Isabel!!!" George and Raynar yelled. All they got was a message,

"I'm with AlaHanDrea, we've gone to rescue Leon, now, y'all be good boys and we may let you out when we get back!"

"Whose idea was it to imprison AlaHanDrea?" George asked the crowd.

"Ya, we should have known that mimic was not her, when we were able to over power her." Braynar said....

"Poor Merrill," Danalli said.

They all looked at each other, then collectively yelled, "Merrill!"

"Well, now, what are you fellas doing all locked up in a cage?" Merrill's image asked them.

He attempted to open the cage door, but could not. His magic was ineffective. He couldn't penetrate the cage at all!

"Wow, there's some serious magic at play here. Who'd y'all piss off?"

"Queen AlaHanDrea, but, she's not nearly as pissed at us as she is at you! Those are her unicorns!

And, she's in love with Leon... Has been since she was only 2 1/2 days old!

She brought Leon to this planet with her!

She's also riding on Isabel on her way to come see you, that's why we called you.

Merrill, she's upset!

Very upset and dude, you may be powerful, but not like she is!

Look here, we don't hate you, Merrill, not even with this stunt you pulled with Leon.

Word of advise, release Leon, send him home and raise a white flag as quickly as you possibly can, before she levels your mountain!" George told the wizard.

"I don't know what kind of stunt y'all are trying to pull, to get me to release Leon..."

"It's not a stunt, Merrill! That girl is pissed off and determined to make a believer out of you!" Raynar was explaining as the ground began to shake.

Only the image of Merrill was in front of them. His person was back at his mountain, which, was beginning to fill with molten lava!

"Ok! Alright! I'm releasing him! Call her off!"

"What makes you think she'll listen to us! It's all up to you now!"

When Isabel and AlaHanDrea reached the island of wizards keep, Leon was standing free on the beach.

When he saw Isabel, he took to the air.

All three of them began the flight back home.

AlaHanDrea jumped from Isabel and landed on Leon's shoulder, grabbing ahold of his mane.

She almost slid off!

It was different landing on a flying lion!

She rolled herself up in his mane to keep from falling.

Leon halted in mid air and began to swell in size!

Power was surging through him as they combined....

She urged him to land so that she could unroll, but Leon was captivated by the amount of power surging through him!

Isabel called out for king Leon to come quick! She sent telepathic messages to George, since it was easier and she was to upset to be understood by anyone else!

"King Leon! AlaHanDrea is trouble! She jumped from Isabel to Leon like she does with the dragons, but his fur made her slide, so she grabbed his mane and rolled herself in it to keep from falling off.

When she does that, it combines her power with his!

He's refusing to land to allow her to let go.

He's draining her of all of her energy!

King Leon, It will kill them both!" George explained with a sense of urgency.

The gate of the cage swung open on it's own.

They assumed AlaHanDrea did it...

King Leon and the others took to the skies to catch up with Isabel and AlaHanDrea.

King Leon was telepathically pleading with his son to land and let her go!

When the group caught up with Prince Leon, they could barely believe their eyes! The already giant lion Prince was huge... combined with her, he was a mega giant!

The energized prince finally listened to his father when he heard him say that he was killing them both!

Reluctantly and drunk with power, Prince Leon landed as soon as he saw a place to safely do so.

They had already begun to shrink back down to normal when he hit the ground.

Braynar, Danalli and Isabel ran to get AlaHanDrea out of his mane.

The exhausted young queen was already unconscious.

Keithen summoned the fairies, they arrived in no time at all and began drumming, creating a circle around Leon.

They drummed the beating of a heart, as Leon laid his head down on the ground, exhausted.

Braynar used his magic to make a hut, grabbed AlaHanDrea up in his arms and carried her inside, demanding everyone leave them alone!

He laid her lifeless body down on a bed he created, then began kissing her. At first, nothing happened, he kissed her again, she stirred. He kissed her with more passion, she began to kiss him back!

"AlaHanDrea, My sweet love, you excite me like none other! You light a fire deep within my soul!" He said, then kissed her lovingly.

Sparks flew!

She stirred.

Then, Braynar heard it... A clap of thunder!

There was an approaching storm!

He picked her up and headed for the storm, followed by Keithen.

"Bro, if it's Sparks she needs, move aside, I can make Sparks fly with her! Give her to me!" Keithen barked at his brother.

Reluctantly, Braynar put her in Keithen's arms, who, wasted no time kissing her. She began to perk right up!

Braynar made a hut around them and left.

"Baby girl, it's me, Keithen... Baby, I love you.

I always have. I've been stupid, I know, but damnit girl, I love you!" He said, then kissed her again, making more parks fly.

The thunder was getting louder, the storm was approaching.

Keithen knew he had to hurry. The storm would save her, but it would kill him! He had to get her up on her feet! So, he started to undress her while kissing her. The heat began to rise!

Keithen didn't want to mess up anymore than he already had with her, so he only took things as far as he had to in order to get her awake and on her own feet.

He helped her outside to a high spot, but once the rain began, he had to go to a place of safety, away from the lightening. The first bolt of lightening seemed to hurt AlaHanDrea!

She turned towards the storm looking angry at it! She hadn't been expecting that first bolt, so it actually hurt when it hit her.

The second bolt was absorbed, as were the rest!

Keithen watched in utter amazement as she absorbed bolt after bolt of high voltage, raw, electricity!

He found it curious that the lightening would hurt her unless she was ready for it. If she were unconscious, he couldn't save her by putting her where lightening would hit her. It would hurt or kill her, just like it would anyone else.

He suddenly felt happy to know that, since he was planning on laying her on the hill if she didn't wake up.

Keithen sat in that hut, thinking about how his kisses awakened her... Thinking about how the Sparks flew between them.

Sparks flew when Braynar kissed her as well, but they seemed more intense when Keithen kissed her.

His thoughts were interrupted by AlaHanDrea walking back into the Hut.

She didn't say a word, she just walked over to him, tip toed, wrapped her arms around his neck and jumped up to wrap her legs around his waist. She sat there, staring into his eyes. He put his arms around her to hold her up, as tho she needed his help for that...

She kissed him softly at first...

Sparks flew when their lips touched.

Keithen couldn't believe the feelings flooding through him... He was loving it, so she kissed him with more passion...

He wasn't sure whether to go ahead or show restraint...

After the kiss, she laid her head on his shoulder, with her legs still wrapped around his waist, so, he just stood there, holding her.. enjoying the minutes with her...

He finally went over and sat on the sofa, still holding onto her. He was going to go ahead and go a little further when he noticed she had fallen back to sleep.

He wasn't worried tho, because it felt like normal sleep.

He heard the drum beat change and knew that Leon was o.k., so he got up as easily as he could and left the hut, allowing her to continue to sleep, while he held onto her.

Isabel smiled and used her magic to put a type of sling around them to help hold her on Keithen, allowing him to be hands free, then had her son get on her back and get a ride home.

It was the first time he'd ever ridden on his mother!

They both loved it!

AlaHanDrea woke up, snuggled up against Keithen, soaring through the air on Isabel's shoulder... She loved the feel of the sling that was holding her against him.

She was thinking that life didn't get much better than that, when Keithen tilted her face up with his finger and kissed her so sweetly... There was so much love in that kiss, that energy pulsed through her entire being.... Isabel sensed it was a special time for them both and took a detour, prolonging their trip....

Chapter 17

Merrill felt like something wasn't quite right when he walked into the room. It was as if someone was there, watching him, but he saw no one.

Still, the seasoned wizard felt a presence.

"O.k. I know you're in here! Show yourself!"

"And just what if I don't want to?" A female voice asked.

"What if I say please?" Merrill asked.

"Well, I dunno about that. I kinda like you not being able to see me..."

"Oh c'mon, don't be like that. You must be here for a reason, are you not?" He suddenly felt a hand on his throat!

"Never, ever, ever pull a stunt like that again, wizard! Am I making myself crystal clear? Compared to me, you have no power! Make no Mistake, I will kill you so dead..." she said, then let him go, but remained invisible.

"Well, hello there, Queen AlaHanDrea, I was wondering when we'd meet again. I'm sorry, I didn't realize the unicorns are yours. They are quite gorgeous and I had not seen anything like them before."

"That's because I brought them with me from Ion 6."

" I see. So, it's not possible that I have even one?"

"No! They are not items! They are creatures! Beautiful, delicate creatures! You can try to befriend them, but that's as far as it goes! That goes for all of my creatures! My centaurs, my fairies...."

"The fairies are yours as well?"

"You'd be best to leave alone the fairies! They look harmless and sweet, but don't be fooled! They possess a very deadly venom! They will not hesitate to make you dead, or much worse."

"What's worse than dead?"

"The fairies can enslave you for the rest of their lives! They turn you into a different kind of creature that obeys them completely. They are dangerous, bitey little devil creatures!"

"Then, why did you bring them here."

"Because they are my family... not by blood, tho I do share some dna... they helped to look after me when I was a tiny baby. "

"Please let me see you. It's not like I haven't seen you before..."

"No."

"Pretty please?"

"No."

"I don't understand why not. I mean, you're here, we are talking.... Can't I at least see who I'm talking to? AlaHanDrea? Are you still here? Well, damn."

The ground began to rumble! Not enough to knock much stuff over, but enough to notice.

"Queen AlaHanDrea, I promise you, I won't hurt them. I will leave your creatures be. Please don't shake the ground!" Merrill was certain the quake was her doing, he wasn't wrong.

The frustrated wizard busied himself searching through his books, looking for a way to deal with a creature as powerful as AlaHanDrea, He felt certain their had to be a way... There just had to be!

"You're not going to find it, you know," a soft female voice startled the weary wizard, who had his face buried in a book of magic.

"AlaHanDrea, I thought you left. I'm so glad that you didn't. Huh, that's strange, I didn't even sense you were still here."

"I'm anywhere and everywhere I choose to be. Tell me wizard, do you have a cure for poisons?"

"For some, I do. Has someone been poisoned?"

"Yes. Me."

"Oh my. Well, that's not good."

"No, not at all good. The rest of me lays in coma, below the surface of the planet."

"Are you asking me for my help?"

"No. I am not. I'm simply making you aware of a situation. How you choose to respond is entirely up to you."

"Ah, testing me..."

"Whatever. Don't flatter yourself."

"Do you know the type of poison?"

"No. It tasted very sweet then very sour..."

"Ah, acelium... That's some bad stuff. Yes, I have a cure for it....

Well, There you are!

Wow! You are even prettier than I remember.... Of course, I will help you. I really am sorry about taking your big kitty like that. What do you say we call a truce and start over? Hi, I'm Merrill Clayton , Wizard extraordinaire... I'm very pleased to meet you, again."

"So says you, witch... wizard... witch...." she replied sarcastically, then said, "Hello Merrill Clayton. I'm very pleased to meet you again as well."

"I look forward to a long relationship with you, your majesty.

For that to happen, we need to gather together some special ingredients and get the antidote made and administered to the rest of you.

I don't think that I can give it to you and it work on the parts that are not with you right now. I'm pretty sure we're going to have to get it down the part of you that is laying in a coma.

The question is, are you going to trust me enough to allow me access to the rest of you?"

"No, that's alright. Healix can administer the antidote."

"Ah, Healix, haven't seen him in ages! Yes, Healix can administer the antidote. He's quite capable. You're a lucky girl to be cared for by him."

"He, Mr Jax and Raynar were appointed my guardians by their father, when I was only 6 years old."

"Oh wow! O.k. so, all three of them are here, on Taurus 9?"

"Sometimes."

"There is one ingredient we may have a bit of trouble finding, then harvesting... It's a special kind of venom... "

AlaHanDrea produced a Brandy glass, pulled her fangs forward and expressed the venom into the Brandy glass.

Merrill was astonished at her having fangs and venom! He took the sample she gave him and checked to see if it was the right chemical make up, being extra careful to not come into contact with the deadly drops of dew.

"Oh my, oh wow, girl, girl, girl! This is some nasty venom you've got here.... Wow!"

"Does it have what we need in it?"

"It may have too much, actually. So, you were created in a lab..."

"Sort of. My parents were created in a lab. I guess you could say I was, too, because my parents met and made me in the lab, they just did it the old fashioned way. They are not of the same species mix. Still, they managed to create me."

"Girl, you have some powerful venom here! Wow! I hope I never piss you off!"

"Me too. Ya, I have to be very careful with my venom. I try to keep my venom sacks drained so it doesn't leak out. I have jars of it stored. I like giving it as gifts."

"Well, anytime you feel that you have too much, I'd be grateful for the gift of it."

"What would you be doing with it?"

"I would take it apart, separate the chemicals. There are some very powerful chemicals contained in your venom. Chemicals that could be very beneficial in other applications.

Some not so deadly applications. Separately, the chemicals are not deadly. It's the combination of the chemicals that make it so deadly.

The chemicals contained in your venom are actually quite beneficial in a lot of areas, especially in the area of medicine."

"Oh really, I did not know that. So does being a wizard mean that you're like a doctor, or a healer... a medicine man?"

"Sort of. I'm an alchemist."

"Oh. You're a scientist."

"I wouldn't go so far as to call me a scientist, because I didn't study science. Not formally anyway.

I'm a wizard.

We come by this talent naturally.

I learned from my father, who learned from his father, who learned from his father, and so on."

"I See. So how are you coming along on the antidote?"

"Almost finished. Can I at least be there with Helix when he administers it? I need to know that it works right, or if I have to adjust the balance, or whatever. In order to do that, I need to take a blood sample."

"And just how do you propose to take a sample of my blood?"

"I'm going to draw it out with a syringe, from your arm probably."

"Okay fine. Here's my arm, take it."

"Ok.... Girl! Your blood is dangerous! It's purple!"

"Well, do your tests!"

"This is going to take some doing.

Your blood contains the seeds of life!

I've never seen anything like it!"

AlaHanDrea thought for a moment, then hollered out, "Healix!"

"Yes? Good to see you, AlaHanDrea. Well, hello, Merrill! It's been a minute! How are you? I see you've met AlaHanDrea."

"Yes. Good to see you, too.

Healix, come look at this, it's the Queens blood."

"Oh, wow! Oh Wow! I hope she doesn't bleed on the dirt!" Healix commented.

"I don't bleed!" AlaHanDrea said, feeling a bit annoyed.

"Well, should you bleed on dirt, there is a very good chance life will grow," Healix told her.

"Show me."

"If I do, the life that grows will be your responsibility." Healix told her.

"Show me."

"As you wish," Healix said, then placed a drop of her blood on a pot of soil.

The soil had smoke rising out of it at first, then a kind of steam. Merrill poured a bit of water on it and it sprouted! A vine began to slowly grow. Tiny leaves began to uncurl... Several branches developed, then the growth became even slower.

A tiny bug flew over and landed on one of the knew leaves... The leaf rolled up around the bug and then the bug was gone!

Merrill pulled out a jar containing flying bugs and put them and the plant in a cage. The plant ate them all, then had a growth spurt.

"Oh wow!" Merrill said in astonishment.

"That's incredible!" Healix commented.

AlaHanDrea just sat, staring at it. Then said, " the antidote please..."

"Uh, ya, sure, the antidote, coming right up!" Merrill commented.

Healix was watching the plant very carefully. The plant was watching him back! He noticed a bulb forming. A tiny little bulb...

"Healix, can I ask you a question," AlaHanDrea said.

"Sure sweetie, what's on your mind?"

"When you come down on a planet to interact with landed creatures, is it all of you, or just a portion? It's just a portion, isn't it?"

"Yes, we are far too large to shrink ourselves that much." Healix explained.

Merrill was taken aback by her question. He'd never really thought about it before. But she had a point, watchers were far too large to shrink down enough... "How fascinating... " Merrill commented.

"I thought so. For you, looking down on a planet is sort of like Merrill looking through his microscope, isn't it?" AlaHanDrea asked, feeling very curious.

"Yes, I suppose it is." Healix told her.

"It's so cool that you can put part of yourself tiny enough to interact with us." AlaHanDrea commented.

"Ya, I suppose it is at that. I rather enjoy the ability to come down onto a planet and interact with the creatures who live on them. Especially this one. I have many friends on Taurus 9."

"So, are there many species in your natural size category? I mean, besides God?"

"Oh yes. This may be difficult for you to understand, or comprehend, well, maybe not for you, but there are universes inside of universes beyond our imagination and comprehension," Healix explained.

"Really? Oh how wild!" She exclaimed.

Merrill was astonished by his answer. He was loving their conversation!

"Ya, that's a good way to put it." Healix said.

"So, there are creatures even larger?" She asked.

"Ya, I suppose there are, but, you're way too tiny to be seen by them, even with the aid of a microscope."

"Oh wow!"

"Child, life is.

It just is.

It's everywhere, in all stages and all categories.

Life is.

It just is."

"So, what about spirits?"

"Ok now, that a very good question. You see, size is only relevant to physical forms, it has no meaning in the spiritual realms.

We are closer to equal in size when we have no physical forms ... "

"Oh wow! That's so cool! Thank you for answering me so openly and honestly "

"My pleasure sweetie. So, Merrill, how's it going over there, are we ready to save this young ladies life yet, or what?" Healix asked.

"Actually, yes, yes we are. Let's go give it a try," Merrill answered....

AlaHanDrea looked so pale, almost dead! It unnerved her to see herself laying there looking so vulnerable like that.

Merrill gave her the antidote. When healix tested it, the awake her passed smooth out.

"I don't think that's supposed to happen," Healix commented.

Merrill looked truly frightened.

Then, the second AlaHanDrea vanished!

Chapter 18

"AlaHanDrea! Just the gal I wanted to see," Leon said.

"Hello Leon," AlaHanDrea said without a drop of enthusiasm.

"Please don't be upset with me. Please? I'm so sorry. I never meant to hurt you... Or me either, for that matter."

"I was already in a weakened state, half of me was in a coma from being poisoned, the melancholy teen queen replied.

"I know and I'm terribly sorry. I've never felt power like that before! Not like that! It was intoxicating! My father said that he has, once, when he flew you into battle. It's really intoxicating!"

"Ya, I suppose it is," she said, with a little melancholy and her voice.

She tilted her head a bit, looking at Leon, then quietly walked over to him and made him start slowly walking backwards, then stopped, wrapped her arms around his neck, pulled herself up and kissed him.

Leon wrapped his arms around her and kissed her back, holding her to where her feet dangled in the air. He set her down and she gently pushed him down into the chair sitting behind him.

It startled him, slightly.

AlaHanDrea climbed onto his lap and kissed him again, this time, reaching down and gently rubbing him through his pants.

He moaned as she touched him and kissed her with far more passion...

She wouldn't allow him to get up out of the chair...

She stood up and slowly pulled her panties down, then off. Leon was trying not to drool! Her top was ever so slowly removed. She climbed back on his lap and made him happy he was a man!

They spent the afternoon exploring one another... Pleasing each other... Bonding...

There seemed to be a bit of a sadness about her. Leon was afraid to ask. He was afraid it would spoil what they were doing, and he really didn't want to risk that!

When AlaHanDrea walked up on Keithen, he was in Dragon state.

"Shift," was all she said to him. He did as she told him to do. Without saying another word, she walked over to him, locked her hands behind his neck and kissed him with love and passion.

He wrapped his arms around her and kissed her back. He gasped when she gently grabbed his crotch, then he picked her up and carried her to his lair...

"Danalli," The sound of her voice startled Danalli.

"Well, hello there, baby girl.... " He was interrupted with a kiss. A very passionate kiss.

"Make Love to me," she whispered in his ear.

He scooped her up in his arms and quickly flew her to his lair.

"Hello Braynar," AlaHanDrea said, startling Braynar.

"Well, hello, sweet girl! Whoa! he said when she dropped her dress and stood nude in front of him. He scooped her up in his arms and carried down into his lair.

"Healix! Hi, what's going on, Raynar's not here at the moment," Isabel told him.

"I'm not here to see my brother, I'm actually here to see you and George."

"You look serious, what's up? OMG, it's AlaHanDrea, isn't it? Healix, what's wrong?

"I allowed the wizard to prepare an antidote for her. I stood there while he gave it to her.

The second he administered it to her, she fainted, then vanished and she's no better. If anything, she's worse, Isabel."

"Is she... Is she... Healix, is she dying?"

"It sure looks like it..."

Tears were rolling down Isabel's cheeks when Keithen showed up first.

"Mom, the strangest thing happened. AlaHanDrea came up to me, kissed me, then seduced me... Then vanished! She never said a word, except to tell me to shift.

Mom, why are you crying?"

"Mom, glad I caught you, the weirdest thing just happened with AlaHanDrea, why are you crying?" Braynar asked.

"Glad I cought y'all all here, the weirdest thing just happened with baby girl, hey, Isabel, why are you crying? What's wrong with everybody?" Danalli asked.

"You all just saw AlaHanDrea?" Healix asked.

"Hey Guys, hey the strangest thing just happened with baby girl, your majesty, what put tears in your eyes?" Kenneth asked, as he walked up to the group.

Ground fog announced the arrival of an angel.

It was Mitchin.

Fear gripped the group when they saw him.

"I guess y'all know why I'm here," Mitchin said, more as a question.

"Is she... Is she?" Isabel stuttered.

"She's still alive. Sort of."

"Well, of course she is! I was just with her!" Keithen said.

"I was just with her," Braynar said.

"Wait, I was just with her," Danalli said.

"So was I," Kenneth said.

"Are y'all talking about AlaHanDrea?" Leon asked as he walked up to the group, "because I was with her, also, then she just vanished."

Mitchin looked at the group and the confused, frightened looks on their faces.

"I think she was saying her goodbyes," Mitchin told them.

"But, Mitchin, how could she have been with everyone at once?" Isabel asked.

"She's just talented that way..." Mitchin told them.

"How, what's got everyone so upset?" George asked.

"George, it's AlaHanDrea, she's dying," Isabel cried, tears streaming down her face. Every one had tears streaming down their faces.

"What's going on," Athena asked as she walked up to the heartbroken group.

"Athena, it's AlaHanDrea. We're losing her," George told her.

"No we're not, I was just with her. She's doing fine! Cheer up already, she's going to be just fine!"

"Athena, we were all just with her, she was saying her goodbyes..." Keithen told her...

"No. No. That's not it at all! I promise you, she's going to be alright!" Athena insisted.

Mitchin went over and put his arms around Athena for a hug.

A super bright light, brighter than anything any of them had ever seen before, except Mitchin, shone from the direction of Healix hide away, where he had AlaHanDrea resting.

Mitchin went down on his knees, so the others followed suit, heads bowed, until the light faded away.

"Mitchin, that was Him, wasn't it?" Isabel asked.

"Yes, it Was! Yes, it was...." Mitchin replied.

"She got a visit from .....?

Healix asked, then was interrupted.

"Ya, she did! One of 2 things just happened... Either He came and personally took her home, or, she's healed." Mitchin and Healix vanished. They left to go check on AlaHanDrea.

She still laid on the bed, motionless.

"But, we saw the presence of God!" Healix exclaimed.

"I know, it makes no sense," Mitchin said, before dropping to his knees.

"I prayed about it," Mitchin said as he stood up.

They watched as AlaHanDrea got up off of the table, while she was still laying on the table. It was a good sign that she was able to separate again. Relief filled both of them as she walked over to them.

"What's up, guys?" She asked.

Just worrying about you, baby girl," Mitchin told her.

"Ya, I had a scary moment. God told me to be strong and fight it. So, that's what I'm doing. He told me that I'm a powerful creature, to channel some of that power, so I did. I'm not well, but I'm better than I was."

"There are a few guys that really need to see you. They think they are losing you," Healix told her.

"They were. Still could. Just not right now. O.k, I will go see them."

She popped in, still out of sight from the group, then separated herself 7 times ...

They all looked at each other and started giggling and chatting. The noise got notice.

"Who is it, Danalli, can you see?" Isabel asked.

"Ya, it's Baby Girl with a whole group of girls!" Danalli exclaimed, then walked over to see AlaHandrea.

He froze in his tracks! So did the rest of the group when they saw all of the AlaHanDrea's standing there, smiling at them.

"Hello everyone. I guess this looks kind of funny to all y'all... I'm sorry for worrying y'all. I wish I could tell you that I'm going to be alright, but I can't do that.

The poison given to me would have already killed any other creature... Thanks to the wizard, I'm not already dead.

The antidote he gave me wasn't quite right, but at least I'm still alive.

Guys, my parents did this to me.

My own parents did this to me.

My own mother and father want me dead.

I saved my mother.

She lives now because of me.

For all intents and purposes, they killed me. It's not their fault I'm still alive."

Tears were running down all of the AlaHanDrea's cheeks.

All of the guys went over and took one of them in their arms to comfort them, even George and Isabel took one.

"AlaHanDrea, I know that they are your parents, but they broke our laws as well as the laws of the humans.

We have warrants out for their arrest. This will not be tolerated!" George told her.

"Thank you, but more than anything, I just need to know why? George, my parents are pretty powerful. Make no mistake! They may appear harmless enough, but they are not. After all, they made me! Don't underestimate them!"

"You're right! I wasn't thinking about that."

"Please don't allow anyone to get hurt trying to arrest them," AlaHanDrea pleased.

"How about we all focus on getting you well," Healix suggested.

Everyone agreed with him.

"I need to say something else. I love you all very, very much! Y'all are my family, not those 2. They made me, but didn't want me from the start.

Y'all have been with me every step....

I love all y'all with all my heart! Each and every one of you! Please, never forget that! I'm not feeling very well, I think we need to rest."

"Do you need to pull yourself back together?" Healix asked.

"No, this is how I'm staying alive. I Must remain separated for now. Please help the wizard! May we please stay with all y'all guys?"

The men all picked one of them up so they could rest in their arms. Raynar had shown up, he and George picked up the remaining 2. Everyone carried their version of her to their lairs and den to let them rest.

Isabel didn't want to leave her side. Thomlin and Franklon volunteered to head up the search for her parents. Healix and his brother, Jax, took off to go help the wizard make a cure.

George and Raynar sat next to their beds, side by side, while Isabel crawled in bed next to her to hold her close. Raynar kept ahold of her hand. He still worried about being absorbed.

"Braynar, I have a confession, I don't want to die."

"I have a confession, too. I don't want you to die!" He crawled in bed next to her and held her close.

"Bray, baby, make love to me."

"Now, sweet baby, you need your rest!"

"No, I NEED YOU! NOW!"

"Yes Ma'am! Are you sure it's a good idea?"

AlaHanDrea opened her top.

"Now, that's not fair!"

She began opening her bottoms. He swallowed hard. "Bray, I need you, I need you now! Energize me! Please!"

"That's right. Sex feeds you! Well, at your service, ma'am! Never let it be said that I failed to do my duty!" He teased, then kissed her with love and passion.

Sparks flew with that kiss. Energy courses through her...

"Keithen, how do you feel about earlier today. I mean, it's the first time you and did that. I was afraid I was dying and I wanted to experience you while I still could."

"AlaHanDrea, I loved it! Sweet baby girl, I loved it! How could I not? I love you! I know I've made mistakes, but, I love you! I'd do it again, right here, right, now if you were up to it."

"Well, get naked then, big guy! What are you waiting for, an engraved invitation?"

Keithen had to laugh when she said that.

"Oh, you precious girl.." he said, then kissed her passionately. Sparks flew like crazy!

Power surged through her, energizing her... Feeding her like nothing else could.

"Leon, you already know that sex energizes me, so what are you waiting for?"

"Who said I'm waiting? Scooch over, I'm a big guy... "

"DANALLI, DOES IT BOTHER you that I split apart?"

"I think it's kinda cool, actually. Now, scooch over and make some room for me. You need some energy and I'm just the guy to give it to you!"

She loved how Danalli was pushy... Taking what he wanted... She loved his aggressiveness...

The magic of his touch sent energy all through her whole being!

KENNETH DIDN'T SAY a word! He just took her to his lair, pulled her clothes off and did what he wanted to do! What he had wanted to do before, and wasn't going to be told no!

She LOVED it!

Everyone seemed to forget what a dangerous creature they were dealing with, They all seemed to lose site of how deadly she could be...

When AlaHanDrea first arrived on Taurus 9, she vowed to get herself a dragon and make him like it...

She managed to get herself an entire flock of dragons and made them love it!

Don't miss out!

Visit the website below and you can sign up to receive emails whenever Jeri Andrew publishes a new book. There's no charge and no obligation.

https://books2read.com/r/B-A-YGIAB-PLFQC

BOOKS 2 READ

Connecting independent readers to independent writers.

About the Author

Retired, I now spend my time writing stories from my imagination, to share with others, to help carry them away to another world, a world of magic and intrigue...